THE SCHOLAR'S KEY

RECKLESS ROGUES
BOOK THREE

ELLIE ST. CLAIR

♥ **Copyright 2023 Ellie St Clair**

All rights reserved.

This book or parts thereof may not be reproduced in any form, stored in any retrieval system, or transmitted in any form by any means—electronic, mechanical, photocopy, recording, or otherwise—without prior written permission of the publisher.

Facebook: Ellie St. Clair

Cover by AJF Designs

Do you love historical romance? Receive access to a free ebook, as well as exclusive content such as giveaways, contests, freebies and advance notice of pre-orders through my mailing list!

Sign up here!

Reckless Rogues
The Earls's Secret
The Viscount's Code
The Scholar's Key
The Lord's Compass
Prequel, The Duke's Treasure, available in:
I Like Big Dukes and I Cannot Lie

For a full list of all of Ellie's books, please see
www.elliestclair.com/books.

CHAPTER 1

Lady Persephone Holloway hated weddings.

This one, however, was an exception.

This was not the finalization of a contract that hardly involved the bride and groom. This was not two people who barely knew one another, who might, in the end, resent one another for tying themselves together in the one life they had to live.

This wedding celebrated the love of two people who were choosing to be together because they couldn't imagine a life apart.

This was a story that she could support, especially when the bride was one of her closest friends, dressed in a white gown so shimmering it was near to silver, a diamond broach gathered beneath the bodice on the front.

"She is beautiful," Percy whispered in Faith's ear. Lady Faith Newfield, sister to the bride and Percy's closest friend, sat stoically watching the proceedings, and Percy wondered if she was seeing anything, for she was barely blinking. "Faith, are you all right?"

Faith nodded, although her jaw was clenched so tightly that Percy was worried for her teeth.

"She will always be part of your life, you know," Percy said. "She will never truly leave you."

Faith nodded again, and Percy leaned over and squeezed her hand. Faith knew that while she only wanted her sister to be happy, Hope's marriage also meant that there would be a great deal of distance between them. If only Faith would be open to marriage herself. But it seemed that was not to be.

Percy leaned in to say something else to Faith but stopped suddenly when a prickling sensation danced over the back of her neck. She was being watched. She looked up to find Mr. Noah Rowley's eyes on her, his brow furrowed behind his spectacles, his mouth in a grim line of disapproval. Percy slunk back in her seat, feeling properly chastised, an uneasy swirl in her stomach.

Very well, then. If the scholarly Mr. Rowley, friend of the groom, Lord Whitehall, felt that she should be silent, then silent she would be.

She would never admit that sitting back and observing the rest of the ceremony was lovely. Hope made a lovely bride with her soft features, golden blond hair and perfect curves. She looked like an angel, contrasting rather wonderfully with Lord Whitehall, as dark featured and surly as Hope was radiant.

It was, however, the happiest Percy had ever seen the viscount.

When the wedding was over, they all made the short journey from the church to Newfield Manor, where the wedding breakfast awaited them. It was a loud event, with all of the chattering amongst the guests, none commanding more attention than Hope and Faith's mother. Percy had always been rather fond of Lady Newfield, even though she

THE SCHOLAR'S KEY

never stopped talking. At least there were never awkward silences when she was nearby.

Cassandra, who had recently become Lady Covington upon her marriage to the earl, was sitting to Percy's right during the breakfast, and when everyone was otherwise engaged listening to a story Lord Ferrington was telling about the last horse race he had attended, Cassandra tugged on Percy's elbow to gain her attention.

"Percy, you know that we have determined where the next clue is leading us."

"Of course," Percy said. Cassandra had stumbled upon a riddle that was tucked inside the pages of a book from her family's estate. She had shared it with the other four of them — Percy, Faith, Hope, and Lady Madeline Bainbridge — who made up their secretive book club, and they had embarked on solving its secrets.

As it happened, Cassandra's brother — Lord Ashford, the future Duke of Sheffield — had found a duplicate copy, and he and his four closest friends, which included Lord Whitehall, Lord Covington, Mr. Rowley and his brother Lord Ferrington — had also entered a treasure hunt. Of course, the initial search had ended well for Cassandra as she had fallen in love with her brother's best friend, Lord Covington, even though the riddle hadn't led them to a treasure but rather the next clue.

It was Hope and Lord Whitehall, who had learned from his father how to break codes, who had solved the next clue. They had discovered a key that they were sure would fit into a necklace set that belonged to Cassandra's family.

The necklace, however, was most likely with Cassandra's aunt in Bath.

"We need to reunite the key and the necklace. I am unsure how, but the necklace is part of this. Since you are going to Bath…"

"You would like me to visit your aunt," Percy finished for her.

"Yes, if you would?" Cassandra said, her expression so earnest that even if Percy had been inclined to say no – which of course she wasn't – she never could have.

"I'll give you the key before we leave Newfield," Cassandra said.

After they had eaten, Percy wandered away to the drawing-room window, taking her drink with her as she looked out at the sea stretching beyond. Newfield was situated on the coast near Harwich, and she wished she had more time to spend here and appreciate the beautiful landscape.

"Are you not having fun?"

Percy turned to find her mother standing behind her, one brow arched. Her mother was a rather quiet woman, yet not in an introverted manner. Rather, when she spoke it was with care that every word had meaning, and she was as curious as Percy about the world around her, although in a much more observant and unobtrusive way.

"Of course I am," Percy said with a genuine smile. "I was just taking a moment to myself."

Her mother turned and surveyed the room behind them. The guests primarily included Hope's family and their close friends. "There are a few single young men here," she said, as they both turned back to face the window.

"So there are," Percy remarked, sipping her drink.

"Are there none that you might be interested in? You have been spending a great deal of time with this company."

"Yes, but—"

She was about to say *why* she had seen them so frequently – because they had come together to solve a riddle which was leading them down a long and winding path of a treasure hunt. One that was likely to come to nothing but was rather fun to participate in, nonetheless. And now, Percy had her own role in the hunt that she was quite excited about.

"It is because Cassandra so recently married her brother's friend. It has brought our circles together."

"I see," her mother said. "Well, there is a certain earl, as well as a future duke among them."

"I am not interested in Cassandra's brother," Percy said, nearly rolling her eyes. She liked Lord Ashford, but he was far from being a strong enough man for her. Percy knew that she wasn't the shy, fair lady that most men sought out. She was still looking for a man who could match her wit, who would challenge her, question her – and she wouldn't be opposed to a man who could lift her and throw her on the bed.

Perhaps she had been reading too many scandalous romantic novels.

"As it is, none of the men here are who I am looking for," she continued.

"Persephone," her mother's face softened. "You know I only want what is best for you."

"And getting married is what is best," Percy finished.

"It is how it is."

"You said I could choose my husband."

"And you can, within reason," her mother said. "But you are already two and twenty, and—"

"And I am running out of time. I know."

Her mother smiled kindly. "Your father is becoming rather impatient, but I am doing my best to keep him happy. He does, however, have a man in mind."

Percy frowned. "He does, does he?"

"Yes. You know his friend, Lord Lecher?"

"Yes…"

"He has a son, Lord Stephen, who will be titled one day."

"I remember him. He tormented me when we visited them years ago."

"Well, he is grown up now, and quite handsome, I am told."

A clattering behind them had them both jumping, and Percy turned around, surprised when she saw Mr. Rowley bent over, picking up his spilled glass from the ground.

"Goodness," she said, bending down to help him. "Are you all right?"

"Fine," he said. "My apologies. Lady Fairfax," he said, tilting his head downward in deference to her mother.

"I shall go find a footman," Percy's mother said, walking away, leaving the two of them together.

Percy reached out to help him with the glass pieces, her hand hitting his when she did – causing a jolt to zing up her arm. She was shocked at first – surely Mr. Rowley wouldn't cause such a reaction within her – but then she saw the blood drip on the floor and realized it wasn't caused by Mr. Rowley at all.

It was from the piece of glass she had cut her finger on.

* * *

"LADY PERSEPHONE, YOU ARE HURT!" Noah swore at himself. Not only had he been listening to her conversation, but then he had clumsily dropped his glass and Lady Percy had injured herself trying to help him.

For an intelligent man, he could be such an idiot.

"It's fine," she said, sucking her finger into her mouth, causing an unwelcome surge of lust to plunge straight to his groin. "Do you, perhaps, have a handkerchief?"

"Of course," he said, reaching into his pocket for one, which she accepted with a smile. While Lady Hope was known to be a beauty, he still thought Lady Persephone Holloway was the most intriguing woman he had ever seen.

And she, in turn, didn't even see him, except as the brother of an earl who was friends with her friend's brother. Hardly an acquaintance. Until he had injured her.

"I took off my gloves to eat," she said, a small smile on her face. "I should have returned them."

"It would have saved your finger, yes," he said, unable to meet her eyes. "Do you need someone to tend to you?"

"It should be fine once it stops bleeding. I have likely ruined your handkerchief, however, even though I asked for it." She laughed, a long, loud laugh that warmed his soul. "I am horrible."

"Not at all."

Far from it, in fact.

No, Lady Persephone was beautiful, vibrant, inquisitive, and everything that Noah could ever admire in a woman.

And, judging from the conversation he had accidentally overheard, not aware that he was even in the room. She hadn't even mentioned him to her mother when denying her interest in the eligible men present. And as for the ideal man she described? Noah was the exact opposite.

"Were you coming to speak with me?"

"Pardon?" Noah said, beginning to panic inwardly.

"You were right behind me when you dropped the glass."

Right. The truth was, he was taking a moment to himself in the corner of the room, and then Lady Percy and her mother had begun talking on the other side of the potted plant. He hadn't wanted them to think that he was listening on purpose, and so hadn't made his escape until their conversation became so personal that he was feeling far too guilty for listening in.

Then his glass had fallen.

"Ah, yes," he said, his thoughts beginning to make sense. "I have heard that we will both be in Bath soon. Gideon – Lord Ashford – has asked me to pay a visit to his aunt, and he told me that Cassandra has asked you to do the same."

"She has," Lady Percy said, surprise on her face. "Do they not trust me, then?"

"I do not think that is it," Noah said quickly. "Perhaps they believe we are best to work together."

"Perhaps," Lady Percy said, although she didn't look convinced. "What takes you to Bath?"

Noah smiled, enjoying this time with her. He wasn't sure he had ever had the opportunity to speak with her alone before.

"Actually—"

"Noah, there you are."

Noah sighed at his brother's voice. He loved the man more than anyone else in the world, but sometimes he truly had the worst timing.

"Lady Persephone, you look as beautiful as always."

Her pink lips tipped upward in a smile that met her eyes as one of her dark curls bobbed down over her temple.

"Thank you, Lord Ferrington. You look quite dashing yourself. You both do," she said, including Noah in her compliment, although he was aware that she was only doing so to be polite.

"You are too kind," his brother said, as charming as ever, and as Lady Percy's attention shifted toward Eric, Noah was reminded that even if Lady Percy wasn't interested in Eric, his brother was, and always would, be the favored one of the two of them.

And it was best that he never forget it, or else the only thing he was going to be was sorely disappointed.

CHAPTER 2

"Richard, you will not be accompanying us?"

Percy took a seat on the wide settee in the corner of the drawing room. She was facing the crimson and gold decorated room but here in the corner, no one could see what she was actually reading.

Their book of the month was certainly not one of which her mother would approve, but she had it hidden within the pages of another. As far as her mother was aware, she was reading a book of poetry which was, in truth, so dry that sometimes she read it when she couldn't fall asleep as it never failed to make her eyes heavy.

"I will not," her brother said. "I have other business to attend to."

"Other business being Lady Jane?" Percy asked, wiggling her eyebrows, causing her brother to shoot her an annoyed look.

"Yes, if you must know, although it has no bearing on you."

"Actually, it does," Percy retorted. "For if she is going to become your wife, then she will be part of our family and I will be spending a great deal of time with her in the future. Do you know how much time women must spend conversing without men? A great deal. And if she is boring or doesn't speak then I will be the one expected to fill the silence and having a one-sided conversation is not ideal. So yes, it does have a great deal of bearing on me."

She lifted her nose as she felt she had won that argument before she returned to her book.

"You're impossible," Richard said with a sigh. "Lady Jane is a lovely young woman from a good family. I cannot see how you would have anything contrary to say about her."

"I wouldn't know as of yet. I do not know her well as she is younger than I am. Which means she is *far* younger than you. She will want to speak of games and dancing and trivial matters whereas you are far more boring and educated and interested in politics and farming and the like."

"Enough, Persephone," her mother finally said, chiming in from across the room where she sipped her tea and read her own book of poetry. Her mother loved poetry. Hence, the reason Percy had to attempt to read this book at some point her mother might wish to speak about it. "Your brother is, at least, interested in marrying. You could learn something from him. Besides, sometimes having different interests can be beneficial."

Richard sent a gloating grin her way, and she rolled her eyes at him when her mother wasn't looking.

The truth was, she would miss her brother when they visited Bath. It had been some time since she had been there, but it was where her aunt lived, and her mother sorely missed her sister. They would spend some time at the baths and taking in the social season there, of course. Percy also had this odd feeling that her mother had another motive for travelling there, although when Percy had asked her – for she always found it best to go directly to the source to determine what she wanted to know – her mother had remained mum on the subject.

"How soon will we leave?" she asked instead.

"In a week," her mother said, to which Percy nodded, as she wondered how she and Mr. Rowley would manage to access this necklace from Cassandra's aunt. As it happened, she was not currently in possession of the key, for Lord Ashford had decided to give it to Mr. Rowley instead.

Of course, he would trust a man over her, even though if there was ever a person one would consider trustworthy, it was Mr. Rowley.

Cassandra had been very clear, however. She felt her Aunt Eve would be much more responsive to Percy than to Mr. Rowley. In fact, Cassandra had implored her to find a way to get the key and then do this all herself.

They could hardly imagine how Mr. Rowley would convince Cassandra's aunt to part with her most prized possession. That was where Percy would come in.

She smiled. She could hardly wait to arrive.

* * *

"Are you certain about this? It is not too late to withdraw."

"Of course," Noah said, crossing his arms as he stood in the doorway of his brother's study. Eric was, both literally and figuratively, born for the role of earl. He was responsible enough to look after all that was required — and quite happy to accept their mother's assistance — while egregious enough to fulfill all of his social obligations.

The only thing he hadn't done yet was take a wife, but Noah knew that was just a matter of time.

"Noah," Eric said, holding out a hand to him in supplication. "You know that you always have a home here. There is more than enough space for the three of us."

"I know that," Noah said. "But soon I'm sure you will find a bride. You do not need a strange uncle lurking about the house, especially once Mother moves to the dower house."

"You are not strange."

"I would be if I lived with you and your family for the rest of my life," he said.

"We have the small estate in Kent. Why do you not live there and look after it?"

"Alone?"

"You would be rather far," Eric considered. "But Bath is even farther."

"It is just for a time, as I further my research. Two or three families have agreed to allow me access to their libraries. After that, I will see you a great deal for we will both be spending so much of our time in London."

"I suppose that is true," Eric said with a sigh. "But do you truly want to spend your life writing about England's history? It seems... dull."

"It is a respectable enough pursuit. I require greater purpose in my life, and since I was spending my time reading and researching anyway, why not do something that has some meaning?

Eric crossed his arms over his stomach and pushed back in the chair as he studied Noah. They both had similar light brown hair slightly touched with curls, but that was where the similarities ended. Eric was tall, rather broad with prominent features while Noah was, in every physical way, a slightly lesser version of his brother.

"We all know how intelligent you are, there is no question there," he said. "I am sure you will write something extraordinary."

"I would like to write a text that is easily read and understood – that will be enjoyed," Noah said. "I am to take primary accounts from all over England and create a volume of books that can be easily accessed."

"How intriguing," Eric said with a pained look on his face. "I'm glad it is you and not me."

"It is fine to be different, Eric," Noah said, which seemed to appease his brother.

"While you are there, you will have another job to do."

"The key and the necklace," Noah said, slightly uneasy about the weight of responsibility upon him. "It means a lot to Ashford to figure this out."

"Well, there is no better man for the job than you."

"Although I am to be aided by a woman, it seems."

"Ah yes, the Lady Persephone."

"Yes," Noah said, not meeting Eric's eyes, for his brother could always deduce exactly what he was thinking.

"Apparently, Ashford's sister would prefer that Lady Percy retrieve the necklace."

"Why?" Noah asked. As far as he was aware, they were to find it together. In fact, he was rather looking forward to it.

"She feels that her Aunt Eve would respond better to a woman. Ashford, however, does not trust her. That's why he gave the key to you."

"He did say that he would prefer I attempt this on my own. I do not see the harm in Lady Percy accompanying me, however."

"Because she will try to take over and do this herself and you—"

"I what?"

"You will allow her to do so," Eric said, although he seemed rather chagrined that he was saying such a thing.

"And just why do you think I would do that, if I have made a promise to Ashford?" Noah asked, raising his brows, attempting not to be insulted.

"Because you fancy her."

Noah balked.

"I do not."

"Don't you?" Eric asked, raising a brow. "You can hardly speak when she is nearby."

"I am not much of a talker. You do enough of that for us both."

Eric laughed at that. "I wish you would show everyone else your sense of humor. You have a greater wit to you than any other man I've ever met."

"You are too kind," Noah said, pushing off from the doorway. "But I do not need anyone else to appreciate such things."

"Noah…" Eric hesitated, and Noah stood still in the doorway, fighting the urge to walk away before his brother said what he knew was on his mind.

"Don't."

Eric stood slowly, as cautiously as he was bringing up this subject of conversation. "It's just, ever since Leticia—"

"Do not say her name. Please. I do not want to speak of this. Especially now, when I am about to leave."

"That is exactly why I think we should speak of it. We have never truly talked about it, never resolved anything. I want you to know—"

"Eric, it's over. Done. You and I are not only brothers, but the best of friends, and I do not want anything to change that. I do not care about what happened."

"It left you a shell of the man you used to be."

"I am perfectly happy with the man I am now. I need you to be too."

Eric was silent, staring at him without saying anything for what felt like minutes, but Noah wasn't about to break the silence. He didn't see a need to.

Finally, Eric sighed and ran a hand through his hair.

"I do not want this next part of your life to begin on a

sour note. Just know that whatever you do, whatever choices you make, I support you."

"Thank you," Noah said, taking a step backward before this continued. "I am going to begin packing. I plan to be gone for a few months so I shall help my valet to ensure all is in order."

"When do you leave?"

"In a week."

Eric sobered. "It is hard to believe you will not be here every day. I'll miss you, brother, you know that?"

"Of course," Noah said, his countenance softening somewhat. "Believe it or not, I will miss you too."

CHAPTER 3

Noah had not been to Bath for years, but so far, he was enjoying himself.

The city was not nearly as large or as dirty as London. He had yet to try the baths themselves, but he had promised Eric that he would do so while he was here — even though he would likely conveniently be too busy. It seemed his brother was worried that he wouldn't take care of himself, but he had nothing to fear.

The very reason he was here was that he was finally doing something for himself. He had spent his entire life in Eric's shadow, and now he was going to do something that made sense for him, that gave him purpose in his own life.

"Well," his Uncle Albert said as he poured a cup of tea from the breakfast tray in front of them, "How are you feeling about your first day?"

"I am looking forward to it," Noah said, reaching for the coffee, which he favored. "I will begin at the Worthington home. They have made Bath their chief residence for years, and I am hoping to find more history on the area."

His uncle nodded, although Noah knew better than to

spend much time explaining his work. Uncle Albert had inherited a bank from his father, Noah's grandfather. It had been something of a scandal when Noah's parents married as his father was to be a marquess and his mother a member of the gentry whose family was in banking, but it had been a match made due to gambling debts on one side and the determination to become as high ranking as possible on the other. A financial transaction, but one that, incredibly enough, had led to a love match.

"One more thing before I forget," his uncle said, pausing in the doorway. He was a wide, broad man who nearly filled it. "Your aunt was quite particular that we take you to the Assembly Rooms tomorrow evening."

"Oh, there is no need—"

"That's what I said, but your aunt is insisting," his uncle said with a shrug as though he couldn't help the decision – which he probably couldn't. His wife was a force. "She said that we must show you the very best that Bath has to offer. She is partial to you, son. I think she wants to entice you to stay."

Noah chuckled at that, although he was already trying to determine just how he could extricate himself from having to spend time at the Assembly Rooms. He had never enjoyed that part of society – making conversation with people he hardly knew. Hopefully, they would have a place where he could hide away and play cards.

"Thank you, Uncle," he said. "For all of your support and opening your home to me."

"Of course. You are always a pleasure, Noah."

"I best go. It's my first day at this library, and I'd like to meet the family before I begin."

"Give my regards to Worthington," his uncle said, raising a glass.

"I will. Thank you again for the introduction."

Fortunately, his uncle didn't live far from the Worthington residence, and Noah chose to walk and enjoy the sunshine Bath had to offer that day. The butler was ready for him and allowed him entrance without question.

"Lord Worthington asked that I see you into the library," the butler said. "He shall be with you momentarily. If you should need anything during your time here, I will be happy to ensure all is in order for you."

"Thank you," Noah said, understanding what the butler was really saying was that they would prefer that Noah didn't wander the house on his own, which he understood. He just appreciated the opportunity to visit what was supposed to be one of the finest libraries in Bath, as the family had kept a main residence here for so long.

He was following the butler down the corridor when a flash of mauve skirts and dark hair caught his eye through a door in the drawing room, and he stopped briefly as the familiarity rushed through him.

He craned his neck for a better look, but he had no time to confirm his suspicions when the door to what appeared to be the drawing room was closed, the butler looking back with a terse look of warning.

It couldn't be Leticia. Not here. Not in this house, just when he was finding his way forward and creating a life for himself.

"In here," the butler said, waving a hand toward the library, and Noah nodded, pulled out of his reveries immediately when he was presented with the room within.

Most men of his station craved a house of a certain stature, be it in the city or country. Noah cared for none of that – except for the library. It was one of the only reasons he would one day like a country home for himself, so he could create a library of this magnitude.

"Mr. Rowley!"

He turned to find a short man with a rotund stomach striding into the room.

"Lord Worthington," Noah said with a small bow, but the man waved him away.

"I am not one for formalities," he said. "Welcome to my home. Tell me, what are you looking for?"

"My uncle said you had letters – primary sources on some of Bath's history."

"I do," Lord Worthington said, walking over to one of the bookshelves at the back of the room, and moving aside a few tomes to find a box behind them.

"These are the letters that I had told your uncle about, letters that my ancestors saved."

"I am grateful."

"You might not be after you see how disorganized they are," he said with a laugh.

Noah nodded, eager to open the box and discover what was within. Lord Worthington must have realized that he had no interest in conversing any further, as he made for the door.

"Well, I'll leave you to it," he said over his shoulder, and Noah opened his mouth to ask him about the woman in the drawing room, but then stopped himself.

What did it matter? She had made it clear who he was to her. He was a pleasure – until someone better came along.

He would save himself much future heartache to remember that.

* * *

"THE HOME IS BEAUTIFUL," Percy said, smiling at her mother as they sat down to tea in the drawing room. She wasn't just saying that to appease her. The house they had taken for their time in Bath was truly lovely, although Percy still wasn't feeling completely at home here. She wasn't certain why.

It was luxurious, welcoming, beautifully decorated, and had ample space.

But it was someone else's home. She supposed it would grow on her in time.

"Have you made any plans for us this week?" she asked, and her mother cleared her throat, somewhat nervously, Percy thought with a frown.

"Perhaps we could attend the Assembly Rooms at least once this week. We have taken out a subscription for the season, and they are so lovely and crowded. Thursday is the fancy ball, which will allow us to see who we might know in Bath this season."

"I'm sure that would be nice," Percy murmured. "Do we know anyone who is here?"

"Your cousins, of course."

"Of course," Percy said, forcing a smile on her face. Her cousins were... friendly, but not the sort of women with whom she usually chose to spend her time. They were always extremely preoccupied with the gossip of the *ton* and the eligible gentlemen. Most women were not interested in scandalous romance novels and brandy. Fashion was the only thing she had in common with most other women.

The butler – who had accompanied them from London, filled the doorway, distracting Percy.

"My lady, your guests have arrived."

"Splendid!" Percy's mother said, clapping her hands together, her eyes flicking nervously toward Percy. "Please show them in."

"Mother," Percy said slowly, placing her teacup back down on the table in front of her. "Who have you invited?"

"Now, Persephone, please be polite," her mother said in a hushed tone, and Percy raised a brow.

THE SCHOLAR'S KEY

"When am I not polite?"

"Just… be cordial."

This was a rather ill sign.

"This isn't Aunt Agnes, is it?"

"Ah, my dear Lady Fairfax!"

Percy stared her mother down as she rose to her feet. She would be polite, sure. But she was going to have a lot to say to her mother once their guests departed.

"Lady Lecher, how lovely to see you," Percy said from between gritted teeth when it was her turn to greet the new arrivals, her stomach dropping when she saw that Lady Lecher wasn't alone. "And Lord Stephen. I didn't know you were going to be in Bath."

Lord Stephen Algate stepped into the room with a smug expression on his face and a privileged air around him. Percy wondered if his stiff, pompadour-styled hair would have moved at all out of place if even the strongest of breezes whisked through the room. She thought not.

"Lady Fairfax, how lovely to see you," he said, bowing low before Percy's mother, who smiled serenely. "And Lady Persephone. You have grown into such a lovely young woman."

His words were cordial, but Percy didn't miss that look in his eyes – nor the way they ran up and down her body as though he was taking in all of the ways she had grown up indeed.

"One does tend to grow over the years," she said before she could stop herself, dipping her gaze when her mother loudly cleared her throat from across the room and stepped forward to intervene, likely before Percy had the opportunity to say anything else.

"Will you have a seat and take tea with us?" her mother asked, stretching her hand out before them. Percy chastised herself for not realizing earlier that there were far too many cakes for just the two of them – and then there were those two additional teacups. It seemed she had to be far more observant when her mother was about.

Lady Lecher took the other chair in the room and Percy's mother sat right in the center of the settee, leaving only the longer sofa where Percy had been sitting. Lord Stephen remained standing, and Percy took a seat on the farthest end as possible as she rearranged her pale yellow skirts, studying him as best she could out of the corner of her eye.

He had a strong jaw, broad shoulders, and could, she decided, lift her and throw her on the bed. Yet the thought of him doing so caused a shudder of aversion to race through her. What was the matter with her?

"Where have you been over the years that I have not seen you at a great deal of societal events?" Percy asked him when the mothers began to make their pleasantries.

"I spend most of my time here in Bath," Lord Stephen said, turning the full vibrancy of his smile upon her. Interesting. Bath was usually reserved for those who could not afford to spend their time in London. "I also enjoy my country home. It is not often that I find myself in London."

"I suppose someday you will have to be more present in London, once you must take your seat in the House of Lords."

"Perhaps," he said distractedly, giving Percy the idea that he was not a man who adhered to much responsibility.

They talked about nothing for longer than Percy would have liked, although she made sure she was on her best behavior for the remainder of the visit. She wasn't above admitting that it would give her a higher ground upon which to stand when she confronted her mother.

As they stood to leave, Lord Stephen leaned in close toward her. "I do hope to spend a great deal of time with you while you are in Bath," he said. "Perhaps we will have the opportunity to become better acquainted."

Percy tried to determine whether there was a hidden meaning in his words, but from what she could tell, he appeared genuine.

"Of course, my lord," she said. "I'm sure our families will enjoy spending time together."

The moment they were out the door and out of earshot, Percy whirled around to her mother, who was standing rather contritely before her.

"Mother!" she said in as even a tone as she could manage. "How could you?"

"How could I what?" her mother said, holding her head high. "I only invited my dear friend to tea."

Percy narrowed her eyes. "I know exactly what you are doing."

"I have no idea what you mean. And I would suggest that you speak to me respectfully."

Percy took a breath, telling herself that aggravating her mother would not help her cause.

"You are trying to arrange a match between me and Lord Stephen."

"I am doing nothing of the sort," her mother said. "Rather, I am introducing you to an eligible young gentleman with a reputable family line. I thought you may wish to come to know him better. You must admit, he is rather handsome, he seems agreeable, and is the kind of man you typically favor."

"That is true," Percy murmured. "But I cannot promise anything. Not yet."

Her mother was right. He was everything she had always said she wanted.

So why did he feel so wrong?

CHAPTER 4

With nothing on their schedule the next day and mercifully no planned visits with Lord Stephen, Percy convinced her mother to accompany her to call upon Cassandra's Aunt Eve – now titled Mrs. Compton, as she had married a second son, which, had been scandalous at the time.

As for explaining her visit, Percy had simply told her mother that Cassandra had asked her to impart a letter to her aunt and to see with her own eyes how she was doing, to which her mother had readily agreed to accompany her.

"Have you met Mrs. Compton before?" Percy asked as they ascended the front steps.

"In our youth, we knew one another," her mother said, her eyes taking on that misty quality that they did when she reminisced. "She was a spirited woman, if I do recall."

"If she is anything like Cassandra, I can imagine so," Percy murmured as she knocked on the door.

"Lady Fairfax, is that you?"

They turned before the door opened to see a woman in

an elegant rose dress with lace adornments standing on the other side of the street, waving frantically.

"Why, it's Lady Westingham!" her mother exclaimed. "I have not seen her in years. I will return in a moment, Persephone. Please do make my apologies to Mrs. Compton and tell her that I will be in shortly."

Percy shrugged as her mother ran off and the door opened, a butler standing on the other side.

"I am here to call upon Mrs. Compton," she said, passing the butler her card. He glanced down at it before opening the door wider and allowing her entrance.

"One moment, please, Lady Persephone," he said. "I shall go tell her that you are here – that both of you are here."

"Oh, my mother is…" Percy began, trailing off as the butler was already walking away, obviously not listening to her. It was not until she glanced behind her that she realized she was not alone in the foyer. "Mr. Rowley!"

"Lady Persephone." He inclined his head toward her. "It appears we have the same idea this afternoon."

"Ah, yes, you decided to call on Mrs. Compton alone, I see," she said indignantly. "Didn't trust me to do the job?"

"As it happens, I have the key," he said, reaching down into a pocket and holding it up for her to see. "I thought it best that I come and see if I could locate the necklace, and then involve you if needed. It seems a job that you shouldn't concern yourself with. I'm sure you have many other obligations."

"Nothing pressing, I assure you," she said, perturbed. This was far more interesting than any social call.

"I might point out," he continued, "that you also came here alone."

"My mother has accompanied me. She shall be here shortly."

"I meant that you came without me, when you promised

you would wait," he said pointedly, to which she sniffed and looked forward, watching for the butler to return.

"Did you really think Mrs. Compton would just hand over what is likely her most prized possession to you?" she asked incredulously, returning her gaze to him. He was leaning back against the wall, his face in shadows, allowing her to study his plain clothes in a slightly faded black.

"I didn't think she would give it to me. That would be foolish," he said, and Percy's spine straightened as she wondered if that was how he saw her. "I only meant to ask her if I could see it — if she does, indeed, have it, as Ashford and Lady Covington suspect she does."

"And what if you determine that the key and the necklace might connect?"

"Then I would distract her while I tried the key."

"How would you do that alone?" she asked, interested in hearing just how he had planned to accomplish such a thing.

"Mrs. Compton will see you now," the butler interrupted, and Percy sprang backward, realizing just how close she had stepped toward Mr. Rowley during their discussion.

As they followed the servant, Percy leaned in to whisper in Mr. Rowley's ear, "I think we should make a plan."

"Together?" he whispered back, and she nodded. "What do you suggest?"

"I shall tell her that Cassandra has told me all about the necklace as I so love jewellery. Especially rubies. Then once she brings it out, I will take a closer look at it and try the key while you distract her."

"How am I to do that?"

"You're a smart man. Think of something."

"That's not really—"

It was too late for their plan to be fully designed, however, as they were led into a drawing room where Mrs. Compton awaited them. She stood in the middle of the room, lengths of gauzy, vibrant fabric flowing off of her body, a turban sitting on top of her head. Her dress lacked any structure as per the style of the day, but it was nothing like the usual pastels that were most often seen amongst the *ton*. Percy recalled Cassandra saying that her Aunt Eve was an interesting character, but she had never said she was eccentric. Percy was now quite excited to become better acquainted with her.

"Lady Persephone and Mr. Rowley, I am told," Mrs. Compton said, her voice melodic. "To what do I owe the pleasure of your visit?"

"We are friends of your niece and nephew, Lord Ashford and Lady Cassandra – well, Lady Covington, I should say now."

"I see," Mrs. Compton said, her brows furrowed. "That still does not explain your visit."

Percy exchanged a look with Noah before returning her attention to Mrs. Compton.

"Cassandra asked me to call upon you, for she would like me to give you a letter."

"A servant could have brought it round."

"Yes, but she had hoped that I could meet you."

"She is checking in on me, then."

Percy grinned, not at all put off by the woman's forwardness but rather enjoying it. "I suppose you could say that," she said. "She also told me about a necklace she believed might be in your possession. I have an eye for beautiful jewellery, especially rubies, and she thought I might be interested in seeing it."

"I see," Mrs. Compton said, eyeing the two of them. "And you, Mr. Rowley, are you here accompanying Lady Persephone? Are you her paramour?"

Percy couldn't help but laugh when Mr. Rowley nearly choked.

"No," Percy said. "We just happened to arrive together. I am accompanied by my mother, although she stopped outside to speak with an acquaintance."

"Then what are you doing here, Mr. Rowley?"

"Just paying my regards," he said as Mrs. Compton eyed him with suspicion, and Percy couldn't help but roll her eyes. However, had he thought he would have managed this visit alone?

"Well, you might as well sit," Mrs. Compton said. "I shall go find the rubies."

"You have them, then?"

She gave them a smile that could only be described as mischievous. "My grandmother always told me that they were to be mine. My mother wasn't so pleased about that, so my grandmother gave them to me directly and always told me to keep it between us." She shrugged. "I guess it doesn't much matter anymore, though, does it?"

"Oh, no rush at all," Percy said. "I did not mean to impose."

"Might as well," Mrs. Compton responded. "I do love showing them off and it has been some time since I have worn them. They will be around my neck, if you don't mind."

That might be a problem.

"I do hope Gideon didn't send you here to ask for them back," she called out as she walked out of the room. "I have heard of the family's financial troubles, but I will not part with these. They were my grandmother's, you know!"

When she was out of earshot, Percy turned to Mr. Rowley, who looked as troubled as she felt. "How are we going to inspect the necklace if she is wearing it?"

"I don't know. We'll have to think of something."

"Your ideas haven't exactly been useful so far."

"Subterfuge is not my strong suit," he muttered.

"So it seems."

He opened his mouth, and Percy found that she was rather anticipating his retort when they heard a scream from overhead. They exchanged a glance once more before hurrying to the doorway of the drawing room in time to see Mrs. Compton flying down the stairs in a rainbow of color, resembling an exotic bird.

"My necklace!" she exclaimed with horror on her face. "It's gone!"

* * *

Noah forgot himself for a moment in his concern, rushing toward the stairs, although he had the wherewithal to stop at the bottom.

"What do you mean, it's gone?" Lady Percy asked, running into him when he came to a sudden stop. When he turned around, she was rubbing her nose but appeared otherwise unaffected. "As in, misplaced?"

Mrs. Compton shook her head, pacing back and forth across the landing at the bottom of the stairs. "I keep them in a locked case in my wardrobe. The case is still there, the lock untampered, and yet, when I opened it, the necklace was gone."

"Where is the key to the case?" Noah asked.

"I keep it around my neck," she said, before smiling ironically. "Isn't that something? It takes the place of where the necklace should be. Some bloody good that did."

In any other circumstance, Noah would have been amused by her cursing.

"There is no other key?" he asked instead.

"There is, but it is hidden in my room," she said. "No one else knows where it is."

"Perhaps a lady's maid?" he persisted, but she shook her

head again, although Noah knew that servants often knew more than their masters could ever imagine.

Mrs. Compton's hand fluttered to her forehead. "I will do a thorough search of the house, but I do not believe it will come to anything. I know in my heart it is gone."

"I can imagine the necklace is quite valuable," Noah said, and her lips formed a straight line, dejection covering her gaze.

"Their value to me is the meaning behind them and what they signify to my family. They were a gift from my grandfather to my grandmother, purchased from her homeland."

"I understand."

Little did she know that there was far more to it – that if the necklace was lost, the path to the treasure might be as well. Noah exchanged a glance with Lady Percy, knowing she was likely thinking what he was – that they didn't want to have to share this news with Gideon or Lady Covington.

"Is it worth hiring an investigator?" Noah asked, and she nodded.

"I will try, although I know better than to raise my hopes," she said, just as Lady Percy's mother, Lady Fairfax, was shown into the house by the butler.

"Mrs. Compton," she said with some hesitation, as she read the tension in the room. "Is all well?"

"Not entirely," Mrs. Compton said with a sigh. "You best come in and I will explain everything. I am sorry, Lady Persephone, that you are not able to see the rubies as you wished."

"It's fine," Lady Percy said with a forced smile. "I am happy to spend time with you and make your acquaintance."

As much as he knew Percy was equally upset about the necklace, Noah ascertained she seemed to be genuine about her intention.

Mrs. Compton had called for tea at the same time that

Percy's mother finally joined them, and they had a pleasant enough visit, despite it being marred by the beginning. When the investigator Mrs. Compton had sent for arrived, Noah, Lady Percy, and her mother stood and made their farewells.

"I do hope we can meet again while you are all in Bath under more favorable circumstances," Mrs. Compton said.

"Please let us know if there is anything we can do to help," Lady Percy said, and they stopped at the bottom of the outside steps. She paused as though she wanted to say something, but Noah knew they couldn't speak freely of the treasure hunt in front of her mother.

"Perhaps we shall see you again, Mr. Rowley," Percy said, intention in her eyes that he knew likely meant she was eager to try to solve this mystery, for he was aware she would have no other reason to seek him out.

He nodded and murmured his farewell, but as he walked away, it was with a weight in his chest, for he knew that they had likely come to the end of their quest.

Which also meant an end to his reason to spend time with Lady Percy – a fact which, he hated to admit, was the worst part of it all.

CHAPTER 5

"Oh, Noah, I cannot wait for you to see the Assembly Rooms. Have you ever been? Perhaps to a concert in the lower rooms? But the upper rooms... oh, the upper rooms where these fancy dress balls are held are beautiful. And you never know who you might see there. Why, once Admiral Nelson was present! I tried to speak with him, but you can imagine the crush..."

Noah's aunt continued to chatter away the entire carriage ride toward Bath's Assembly Rooms. He shifted uncomfortably, the squabs squeaking with the change of his weight overtop.

The truth was, he would prefer to be just about anywhere else right now than going to socialize with Bath's highest society.

Well, almost anywhere.

He wondered if Lady Percy was going to be there and then pushed the thought from his head. This was going to be a long stay here in Bath if he was going to be looking for her everywhere he went.

"I cannot wait to introduce the brother of an earl to all of them!"

"I'd prefer you didn't," he heard himself saying, stopping his aunt mid-soliloquy.

"Didn't what?"

"Introduce me as such. Your nephew, Noah Rowley, is perfectly fine."

"But—" Her eyes were wide, as though she was incredulous that he would not want all to know of his family's connections.

"I believe Noah would just like to be known for who he is and not for who his father was or his brother *is*. Is that not right, son?" his uncle softly interjected, and Noah nodded gratefully.

"That is exactly right."

"Well…" his aunt said, and Noah felt a twinge of guilt for having deflated her excitement.

"You can tell them of the work that Noah is doing," Uncle Albert said, and that somewhat brightened her spirits, although she was not nearly as excited as she had been before.

By the time they arrived, the fancy dress ball was already well underway, and as they started up the stairs, Noah was immediately surrounded by the overwhelming floral perfumes and smoke that clung to the fabrics of their wearers. It was a plethora of pastels, interspersed with the dark wear of most of the gentlemen and the brightness of a few dandies.

Noah had worn as indiscreet garments as possible, hoping to blend in with everyone around him. He adjusted his spectacles after he was shoved from one side, sighing as he wished the person would know of his ire, although he wasn't about to say anything.

He stepped through the doorway, and upon seeing the large room in front of him, he was, at least, able to appreciate just why his aunt was so eager to show him the place. The ballroom was wide and open, the musicians playing from a balcony above him. He looked up to see them behind the railing, backdropped by the light blue ceiling with its white crown moulding that reminded him of the sky on a sunny day, interspersed by fluffy white clouds. Chandeliers hung down from the ceiling, lighting the room and dazzling all who stood below them.

He wondered how any woman could ever compete with its grandeur.

But then he saw her and knew that there would always be one who could do so.

To Noah, it seemed like the crowd before him parted like the Red Sea to provide him a tunnel through which to see her. Lady Persephone, resplendent in a pale pink gown, her dark brown hair high on her head above it, was speaking animatedly in front of two women he guessed were her family members by the way they leaned in and interacted with one another, although he couldn't know for certain.

Lady Percy flung back her head and laughed at something one of them said, and he loved how she was able to give herself over to emotion without worry about what anyone might think of her.

He hated the part of himself that wished *he* was the one who was making her laugh.

But that was not him. He didn't have such a sense of humor. Sure, Eric found him amusing, entertaining even, but Eric was his brother. They knew one another better than nearly anyone else, so it made sense.

He wasn't going to fool himself that Lady Percy would feel anything for him but vague interest as an acquaintance.

It didn't matter what he told himself, however. When a tall, broad man stepped up to the small group of women and bowed in front of them, his eyes heavy on Lady Percy, Noah was reminded of what kind of man she preferred.

"Uncle," he said, leaning over and interrupting his uncle before he could stop himself, "who is that man over there?"

"Where's that?"

"Across the room, with the group of young ladies."

His uncle squinted, but it was his aunt who answered.

"Oh, that is Lord Stephen, son of Lord Lecher," she said. "He has resided in Bath for quite some time, I believe. From what I've heard, he is finally on the hunt for a wife. Looks like he is beginning his quest."

So he was. With Lady Percy.

"Do you know him, Noah?"

"I do not," he said, throwing back his drink. But he did want to know just what Lord Stephen's intentions were for the woman who Noah couldn't stop thinking about – whether he liked it or not.

* * *

Percy forced a smile on her face.

Lord Stephen was affable. He was polite. He was from the correct bloodlines and was in line for a title.

He was physically strong and commanded attention. He was the perfect combination of what attracted her and what her parents wished for her.

So why did she wish him to finish this story he was telling and walk away from them all?

Suddenly she realized all eyes were on her, waiting for her to say something, and she cleared her throat, wishing she had paid more attention.

"Percy does love to dance," her cousin, Elizabeth, said, taking pity on her and elbowing her in the side.

"Yes," Percy said with a smile. "I do."

"And would you like to dance with me?" Lord Stephen said.

"I would. Yes," she lied, but it would be incredibly rude to say no — even for her.

"Very well. I shall collect you shortly when the next dance begins. Ladies," he said, bowing slightly to all of them, and Percy's lips tightened together.

She took a sip of her drink as her cousins began tittering about his interest in her, pausing when her gaze fell upon a familiar figure across the room.

Mr. Rowley.

If she didn't know him better, she likely would have missed his figure entirely, as he seemed to fade into the background behind him.

Well, not literally, for he was wearing dark trousers and a dark jacket, and the wall was sky blue, but suffice it to say, he certainly did not stand out – mostly because of the aura around him, one that made it seem as though he was trying to hide.

Their gazes caught and held, and there was something in his eyes that interested her – although she couldn't have said exactly what it was. She raised an eyebrow in question, and she could have sworn his cheeks reddened as he lifted his drink and turned away.

"Who are you looking at?" Elizabeth asked.

"A friend," she said, an involuntary smile striking her face. Mr. Rowley had become rather entertaining, whether or not he meant to be. "A friend of a friend, I suppose I should say."

"You seem rather interested in said friend," said her other cousin, Rebecca, peering around Elizabeth to see him. "I do not see anyone."

"He is standing right there," Percy said, pointing.

"I only see women."

"Rebecca. He is right in front of you."

"Oh, him — in the spectacles?"

"Yes," Percy said in exasperation, turning away from him when he began to look their way once more. "Now will you quit staring? I do not want him to think that I am gossiping about him."

"Is there anything to tell?" Elizabeth asked, not listening to Percy at all, rather shifting around her for a better look. "He is rather handsome, actually, in a rather unconventional way."

"Handsome?" Percy said in surprise. "I suppose he is pleasant looking." She hadn't considered his looks. He was just... Mr. Rowley.

"And here I thought perhaps you had a penchant for the man the way you were looking at him," Elizabeth laughed. "I see I am wrong. Will you introduce me?"

"Introduce you?" Percy repeated, rather stupidly. She should. Why wouldn't she? Mr. Rowley would be an appropriate match for a woman like Elizabeth, with noble connections but no direct link to a title. And yet... the thought of doing so left a rather uncomfortable swirling sensation in her stomach. "Yes, of course," she said, ignoring her fickle, confusing emotions. "Let us go."

She led them across the room, Mr. Rowley looking from one side to the next as they approached, as though he was wondering who they might be seeking out, not believing that it could be him.

"Mr. Rowley, how good to see you," Percy said when they reached him. Now that Elizabeth had said it, she was unable to prevent herself from looking for the handsomeness that her cousin had mentioned. Perhaps, beneath the spectacles, the hair that he wore in a style that was some years out of date now, the drab clothing, and those sideburns that were rather—

"Lady Percy," he interrupted her musings. "You look lovely tonight."

"Thank you," she said, struck by the heat that climbed up her cheeks.

"Percy always looks quite remarkable," Rebecca said, stepping forward. "She is the most intelligent of all of the styles of the season."

"I enjoy clothing, is all," she said, rather flustered, as one of her cousins – she wasn't sure which – poked her in the side. "Oh, yes, my apologies. Mr. Rowley, please meet my cousins, Miss Elizabeth Paulson and Miss Rebecca Paulson."

"Lovely to meet you," he said, bowing slightly.

"How do you know one another?" Elizabeth asked, looking back and forth between them.

"We met through common friends," Percy explained, to which Mr. Rowley nodded.

"What do you do with your time, Mr. Rowley?" Rebecca asked, and Percy knew that it was not so much that she was interested in what he did, but to whom he was connected.

"I am studying and writing the history of England from the time of the Acts of Union," he said, which immediately lost some of the interest of Percy's cousins. Percy smiled slightly to herself, for if they knew the truth – that Mr. Rowley was currently in line to inherit an earldom, should anything happen to his brother – they would not be so disappointed in him.

But if Mr. Rowley didn't see fit to share that information, then neither would she.

"Mr. Rowley—" she began, but then stopped, her mouth dropping open.

"Percy," Elizabeth hissed in her ear after she said nothing for a few moments. "Percy, you are gaping like a fish."

"Yes, Percy," Rebecca said, only she did nothing to quiet her words. "Do close your mouth."

Mr. Rowley, however, said nothing. He only turned to see what had so captured her attention.

And when he returned his gaze to hers, it was wearing the same astonishment that Percy felt.

"The necklace," they said together. It appeared they had found it, without even trying.

CHAPTER 6

Noah had to tamp down the urge to rush over and ask the woman just where she had received such a beautiful – and valuable – piece of jewellery, but first, they had to rid themselves of Rachel and Emmaline or whatever the names of Percy's cousins were.

He usually prided himself on his memory. But it was hard to retain information regarding anyone else when Percy was standing in front of him.

Percy stuttered for a few moments about a necklace that she admired on a woman across the room. It appeared she felt that, in this instance, the truth was best. Her cousins wouldn't stop asking to which woman she was referring until Noah realized that they were perhaps missing an opportunity – the opportunity to determine just who the woman was, and whether the jewels around her neck could be those that they were looking for.

"The woman over there – the dark-haired one in the crimson dress with rubies about her neck," he said. "Who is she?"

Percy shot him a look as though he was giving away too much, but the taller cousin leaned in with a gleam in her eye.

"*She* is Mrs. MacNall."

"Mrs. MacNall?" Percy repeated, raising her eyebrows.

"She is…" The two sisters looked at one another.

"How do we say it?"

"In a polite way."

"It is almost shocking she is here, we shall say that."

"I can hardly believe she was allowed in."

"Enough," Percy said, likely louder than she intended. "Neither of you is any less innocent than I am, so you might as well just say what you mean instead of skirting around it."

"Very well," the shorter one said, rolling her eyes. "Mrs. MacNall is a…" She dropped her voice. "A fallen woman."

"But a well-kept one," the taller one – Evangeline? – said with a tilt of her head.

"Don't get any ideas," her sister murmured.

"Of course not!" the other trilled.

"Is she attached to a man?" Noah interjected, and they looked at him almost as though they had forgotten he was there.

"I believe she is. She has her own house, just off Kingston Road. Oh, who was her protector again, Elizabeth?"

Elizabeth. He had been close on the name.

"Lord Chesterham, maybe?"

"Oh, yes, that's him."

"He is married, is he not?"

"He is."

"Scandalous."

"That she is here. Not that he has a mistress. Everyone does."

"Yes, that's right," the tall one — Elizabeth, said. "He does not make a secret of it."

"No," Rebecca said, shaking her head in disapproval. "One should keep such a woman behind closed doors."

Noah took a step back from the chattering women, seeing that Percy was doing the same thing. She stepped around her cousins to come over to his side.

"We need to speak with her," she said in a loud whisper.

"I think you should do it. She is far more likely to speak to another woman."

"I'm not sure," Percy said, nibbling on her bottom lip, which Noah tried to ignore as it was causing him to feel all kinds of things that he really should ignore. "She might be more inclined to speak to a man."

"I've never had much luck convincing a woman of anything."

That sounded rather like he was feeling sorry for himself, which he didn't think Percy would appreciate. He cleared his throat. "I do think you should try first. You have a way about you."

Her eyes widened as she arched back slightly away from him. "What does that mean?"

Why had he said such a thing? Now he had to explain himself.

"You are a… charming woman, Lady Percy," finding that he was no longer able to look her in the eye.

"Thank you," she said, although she continued to stare at him with either interest or concern – he couldn't be sure which. He supposed it wasn't often that he paid any woman a compliment, and he had certainly never spoken as such to Lady Percy.

"Very well," she said finally with a shrug. "I will try. Although I will have to be careful, for even my mother, who is rather forgiving, would not be pleased if I publicly make the acquaintance of a woman considered scandalous. I shall wait until she leaves the ballroom, and then see if I can follow her."

"Do you need anything from me?"

"I shall be fine, I'm sure," she said, and Noah couldn't help how drawn he was to the confidence she exuded.

"Oh, there she goes," Percy said with excitement before leaning in toward her cousins, who were in the midst of a conversation or argument – he couldn't be sure which. "Excuse me. Elizabeth, Rebecca, I shall return in a moment."

And with that, she hurried away in a flurry of pale pink skirts, Noah watching after her.

* * *

MERCIFULLY, Percy was able to leave the ballroom without anyone stopping her – most notably her mother, who she was sure would want to accompany her, even if it was to the ladies' room. Mrs. MacNall entered the small room, and Percy waited, rather impatiently, outside for her to emerge. A small line formed behind her, and when Mrs. MacNall came out, Percy left her place to follow her. When they were out of sight from any prying eyes, she increased her pace a few steps and reached out to touch the woman's elbow.

"Mrs. MacNall?"

The woman turned, looking down at Percy as she did. She was tall, her face artfully made up to enhance her beauty without appearing artificial. Her gown was as grand as any other lady's in attendance. She must be paid well to afford such garments if Elizabeth and Rebecca were correct as to her profession.

"Yes?"

"You look lovely this evening."

The woman simply arched a brow, clearly not interested in any pleasantries, but quite correctly rather suspicious.

"Do I know you?"

"You do not," Percy said, deciding the truth was best in this instance. "I just arrived from London."

"I see. Do you know who I am?"

"No, I have yet to make your acquaintance." So much for telling her the truth. "You have exemplary fashion sense. The velvet crimson you are wearing is simply divine. And your necklace is breathtaking. I was drawn to it."

The woman raised her hand to the jewels around her neck. Now that Percy was able to take a closer look at them, she was sure they were those that belonged to Mrs. Compton.

"Thank you."

"I love rubies."

"As do I."

"May I have a closer look?" she asked, leaning in, but Mrs. MacNall shifted back away from her.

"I must return to the ballroom."

"My apologies. I could not help myself, for they have so captivated me," Percy said, but it appeared Mrs. MacNall was not interested. However, in the brief moment Percy had leaned in, she had seen what she had been looking for – the Spanish inscription. It had to be the Sutcliffe family jewels. But how had they escaped from Mrs. Compton's locked box to come to rest on the neck of Lord Chesterham's mistress?

She didn't have time to ask any further questions, for without another word, Mrs. MacNall turned and walked away from her. Percy sighed, knowing that continuing would be fruitless. She was going to need Mr. Rowley's help after all. She began her return to the ballroom when a tall, imposing figure blocked her way.

"Lord Stephen," she said in surprise when she tilted her head up to see who had so invaded her space. "How… nice to see you again this evening."

By nice, she meant inconvenient.

"I am glad I found you. I was hoping to have a moment to speak with you alone."

"I am not sure that is proper, Lord Stephen," she said, even though she didn't care much for propriety, but more so sensed an urgency to accomplish what she had come here to do.

"It will be but a moment," he said, stepping to the side to block her path when she tried to move around him. "I hope you have come to realize, Lady Percy, that you intrigue me."

"I do strive to be intriguing," she said lightly.

"I am not sure if you are aware, but I am interested in taking a wife."

"You say that as though you can walk into the general store and buy one," she said, to which he smiled slyly.

"And yet, here we are, in a building where so many eligible young ladies are laid out in front of me, their merchants—pardon me, *mothers*— prepared to share with me all of their qualities as to why I should consider them. Which makes me wonder… is it that you have a deficiency, or are you simply not available for sale?"

Percy stood tall in front of his offensive words.

"As it happens, Lord Stephen, I do not consider attaching myself to a man for the rest of my life to be a contractual obligation. If that is what you are looking for, then I would suggest that you find another besides me."

"So challenging," he murmured, his eyes sweeping up and down her body. "Perhaps that is what has scared others away."

"This conversation is finished," she said firmly. "Excuse me."

She made to sweep past him, but he blocked her path once more. She feinted to the left, and when he went to stop her, she deftly stepped back and around him.

He reached out, his fingers encircling her arm, but just when she was about to tell him more clearly to unhand her, they were both stopped by an interrupting voice.

"Lord Stephen, is it?"

Relief swept over Percy when Mr. Rowley stepped in between them, his presence causing Lord Stephen to take a step backward, dropping his hand to the side. He might be persistent, but he was not foolish enough to be caught entrapping a woman against her will.

"Yes."

"I am Mr. Noah Rowley. I believe you know my brother."

"Do I?"

"Lord Ferrington."

"Ah, yes, of course," Lord Stephen said, even though it was obvious he had no idea to whom Mr. Rowley referred, but he was certainly not going to refute any claim when the man was titled.

"He sends his regards," Mr. Rowley said, before inclining his head back toward the ballroom, obviously telling Percy to continue. She hated to allow another to fight her battles for her, but she also knew that this was her best opportunity to escape.

"Good evening, Lord Stephen, Mr. Rowley," she said with a slight curtsy before walking away, even though she was most eager to capture Mr. Rowley to speak to him about the necklace.

She wanted to share what she had learned – and just what she now needed him to do.

CHAPTER 7

Noah was cursing himself after his encounter with Lord Stephen. He should have told the man just exactly what he would do to him if he continued his pursuit of Lady Percy with such unsavory intentions, but then, who was he to defend her? An acquaintance? Friends of mutual friends? Besides that, it was not as though he was going to challenge the future marquess to a brawl or a duel.

He had no chance to win either.

So instead, he had taken his leave, seeking out Lady Percy once more, but it seemed by the time he returned to the ballroom that she had disappeared.

He was about to leave himself when he felt a tap on his shoulder and turned around to find her there.

"Ask me to dance," she whispered, and he looked around, already assuming she was speaking to someone else.

"You want to dance with me?" he said when he didn't see anyone about, and she rolled her eyes.

"Yes. Why else would I ask you? I need to speak to you."

Ah, yes, the necklace. He had nearly forgotten about that.

The musicians struck up a waltz, and he held his hand out

to Percy, leading her onto the floor, as a scent that reminded him of the cherry blossom orchard at his brother's estate washed over him. He settled one hand on her waist, taking the other in his hand, as he attempted to remain unaffected at the heat of her palm against his through her gloves.

"Were you able to speak with Mrs. MacNall?" he asked, his eyes looking about the ballroom over her shoulder.

"I spoke with her," she said with a sigh, her breath against his neck causing him to shiver. She was the perfect height in his arms, her head in line with the crook of his shoulders. "Unfortunately, it came to naught. She had no interest in speaking with me, let alone allowing me to see the necklace. However, I was able to come close enough to it to see the Spanish inscription. It is the necklace we are looking for, Mr. Rowley, I know it."

"Call me Noah."

"Pardon me?"

She leaned back away from him, her beautiful blue-green eyes searching his face. It rather disconcerted him, but he allowed her to do so as he also couldn't look away from her.

"With our common goal and the time we are spending together, I am happy to have you call me by my first name," he said.

Primarily, he wanted to hear it on her lips. He hoped his reasoning would be acceptable.

"Very well, Noah. You may call me Percy."

"Do you prefer it to Persephone?"

"I do," she said, looking up at him from beneath her dark lashes. "Persephone sounds so formal. And of course, it is difficult to say. When my brother was a child, he couldn't say it, so he said Percy instead and the name has stayed with me ever since. Only my mother calls me Persephone."

"Bringer of death."

"Pardon me?"

THE SCHOLAR'S KEY

"The name Persephone is Greek," he explained. "It means bringer of death."

"Lovely," she said with an undercurrent of sarcasm, and he realized she didn't appreciate his explanation but she couldn't help herself.

"Actually, it is," he said. "She was said to gently guide and comfort those descending to death. Interestingly, she personified duality, for while she was the wife of Hades, she was also the daughter of Zeus and Demeter, and was the goddess of regrowth, spring, and vegetation."

"You are a man of much information."

Noah took a step backward, his face warming as he had been caught up and said far more than he had meant to, as he often did. He cleared his throat and attempted a simpler tactic.

"Percy suits you."

She beamed, and warmth blossomed from deep inside him that he was the one who had caused such a reaction.

"Now, Noah, I believe you have a much better chance of convincing Mrs. MacNall to show you the necklace. Also, do you know Lord Chesterham?"

"In passing."

"Would you be able to speak with him? Ask him where he purchased the necklace? It must have been stolen and he then bought it for Mrs. MacNall. Unless she has another protector. Does a woman only have one at a time?"

She looked at Noah with such conviction in her eyes that he would be able to answer the question, but he hardly knew what to say.

"I-I wouldn't know. I have never paid such a woman, nor do I have any close acquaintance with a man who has."

"Oh." Her lips formed a round pink circle. "I suppose that is commendable."

"I hope so."

"I know Lord Chesterham in passing," he said, answering her initial question. "I believe he enjoys the card room. I will join a game with him and see if I can uncover any answers."

"Good," she said with a nod. "Just be sure you do not ask him directly if he bought them for her."

"How else am I supposed to ask?" he said, furrowing his brow.

"You will have to think of something, but the man is married, so you can hardly ask if he bought a gift for his mistress. Perhaps say you are considering buying rubies for a woman and would like to know where to find them."

"That is a good idea," Noah mused, tilting his head to the side, and Percy laughed as though amused that he would have considered it to be anything else.

"Now, as for Mrs. MacNall..." Percy pressed her lips together, looking over his left shoulder. "You will have to try flattery. See if you can get close. Impress her with your connections."

"But—"

"I understand, you do not want to be known by your brother. But in this case, you might have to try it. Fortunately, she is alone and at the refreshment table at the moment. You could speak to her without it appearing that you are having a private conversation."

"Very well."

"Best of luck, Noah. I know you can do this," she said as the song came to an end and he reluctantly released her, having enjoyed her proximity far more than he should have.

He turned from Percy, not knowing how else to part with her, and took in a breath as he looked for the woman, finally seeing her over by the side of the room. He would far prefer to retreat to the card room first to see if he could locate Lord Chesterham, but he was aware that if he didn't do this now, he might lose both his opportunity and his nerve.

He hurried over before she walked away, leaning over to pick up a glass of pale yellow liquid, unsure exactly what was in it but guessing it was lemonade. He was not a fan. Far too sweet and syrupy for his liking.

She was standing next to the table, looking out over the dancers now. Noah stood beside her facing the table, needing to speak to her but not wanting to attract too much attention.

"Mrs.—" but he wasn't to know who she was. "My—" She was not a lady. He should not refer to her as such. "Excuse me, there."

She didn't turn, and he realized he was not being loud enough. He cleared his throat. "Madam?" Oh dear. Now she might think he was calling her a madame.

"Are you speaking to me?" she asked, turning dark eyes upon him, although they were not without interest. He swallowed at the attention.

"Yes."

"What can I do for you?"

"I—that is—you look lovely."

She lifted an artfully defined brow. "Thank you."

"Are you—that is, do you have a gentleman?"

She appeared vaguely amused. "You will have to be more clear."

She was not making this easy on him. He tried to take a closer look at the necklace, but his cheeks warmed when he realized that by doing so, she assumed that he was looking at her ample bosom – although she didn't seem to mind. He pushed his glasses farther up his nose.

"Are you here – at the Assembly Rooms – with a man?"

"Not particularly," she said. "Why do you ask?"

"I—that is, my brother is an earl, and he has suggested—" What did his brother suggest? Why would his brother have anything to do with this? Percy had told him to mention his brother but now this was all muddled.

"Tell you what," she said, leaning in close. "If you would like to find me later – whether that be tonight, tomorrow, or the night after that, then come to the Queen's Hand."

"Where is that?"

"Ask around — you will find it," she said with a smile that was both suggestive and amused. "But Mr....?"

"Rowley."

"Mr. Rowley. I do not do this entirely for my finances. I also do this for my enjoyment. And I like a man who can entertain me. We shall see if you have it in you."

He swallowed hard, not liking where this was going. How was he to tell Percy that he had not only failed tonight but had no chance in the future?

"Goodnight," he said, uncertain what more there was to say, and turned around to find that there was no need to tell Percy anything, for she was standing just a few steps away, behind one of the columns of the room so that she was invisible to Mrs. MacNall. Once the woman in question had moved away, Percy stepped out, expressionless.

"Noah."

"Yes."

"That was..."

"Painful, I know."

"Yes, that was one of the words I was going to use for it." She sighed. "If you must be entertaining for her to notice you, then we might be in trouble."

She was nothing if not blunt.

"Do you have a suggestion?"

She stopped, tapping a finger against her lips. "I do."

"Which is?"

"I am going to help you."

"Percy, you cannot go to such a club."

"Of course not, although it is rather annoying that *you* can do so without censure."

"That is not my fault."

"No, but that is something we can discuss another day. Now, as for your appointment tomorrow night. I might not be able to attend with you, but I can prepare you."

"How will you do that?"

"I will give you instructions and help you to practice."

"What? When? How?"

She only laughed, further disconcerting him, for he had been asking the questions out of serious interest to know just what to expect from her.

"Call upon me tomorrow. I will think of a way that we can spend time alone together, without my mother. We have work to do, Noah!"

Then, with a spring in her step and a smile on her face, she walked away, and he only wished he could be as hopeful as she.

But he knew himself far better than she did.

And he was liable to be a complete disaster – with Mrs. MacNall, yes, but even worse, with Percy herself.

He wished he had never agreed to this, for there was only one place it could lead to.

Disappointment.

CHAPTER 8

*P*ercy hadn't been this excited since it had last been her turn to select a book for their scandalous club.

She had never told the four friends who formed part of the club with her that she had spent hours at the circulating library, hidden where no one could see the titles in her pile, reading a few pages of many different books to try to decide which they would all most enjoy.

Now she was waiting for Noah to arrive with the same anticipation. She had been impressed with his attempt to speak with Mrs. MacNall yesterday. She could tell that it wasn't easy for him to approach strangers, most particularly a woman with such experience who could very likely ascertain that Noah was not a man who was well versed in seeking out such company.

Or maybe he would, she thought with a shrug. It was hard to know with a man who remained so closed off from others. Sometimes she would just love to look inside that head of his and discover what was happening, what was driving his responses and his actions – but she knew better than to ever

THE SCHOLAR'S KEY

ask, for she guessed he would keep that to himself. Besides, it was kind of fun that he was such a mystery.

"Persephone, I am leaving now!" her mother said, and Percy rushed to the door with quick steps, eager for her mother to depart before Noah arrived. If her mother was gone when he came, then she would have no reason to suspect a thing and Percy wouldn't have to explain his visit. "Are you sure you do not want to accompany me?"

"I am far too tired from yesterday. I do hope you have fun, however!" Percy said, feeling bad about the lie but eager that her plan had a chance of working out.

She had ideas for Mr. Rowley – ideas that she was sure would make him most attractive to the skeptical Mrs. MacNall.

A knock sounded, and before Percy could think of what she was doing, she was rushing forward to the entrance, opening the door before the butler could.

"Noah!" she said with a grin when she saw him standing there, hat in hand, his expression all kinds of concern. "You came."

"You didn't give me much choice," he murmured, and she reached out and pulled him into the house before he could decide to leave.

"There is nothing to be worried about. We will have a lovely time. I promise," she said, hoping that she was telling the truth and he would, if nothing else, enjoy his time with her. "Come along to the back parlor. I have asked my maid to meet us there so that we will not be completely alone."

"Very well."

"I also have my father's valet joining us."

"Whatever for?" he asked, tugging slightly on her hand, and it was only then she realized that she was still holding onto it. She dropped it, unsure if he enjoyed such close touch.

"He is skilled in grooming."

"Grooming?" They entered the parlor now, and when he removed his cloak, she realized that she hadn't even given him time to provide his hat and cloak to the butler. No matter.

"Yes," she said with a smile, folding her hands in front of her. "For your hair."

"What's wrong with my hair?" he asked, running a hand over it as his brow furrowed.

"It is…" She wasn't sure how to convince him to change it without insulting him. "It is very suitable for you, but for Mrs. MacNall, I think we should slightly change it."

"You do not like it."

"I like it just fine," she said, "and afterward if you would like to return to it, then please do so."

"Very well," he grumbled.

She began to circle him. "Your spectacles make you look rather distinguished, so they can stay."

He snorted. "They were never an option. I can hardly see without them."

"For your dress, I have invited Bath's finest tailor to visit you tomorrow."

"Percy—"

"You do not need much from him, and I have told him what to style for you," she said. "Then you should be ready in that regard."

"I hadn't realized that there was any issue in how I look," he said wryly, clearly insulted.

"There is nothing wrong! Nothing at all," she said hurriedly. "We just do not want you looking so… respectable."

"Very well," he said, although he appeared somewhat placated.

"Mary, there you are," Percy said as her maid came in the

door, her timing fortunate for Percy no longer had to explain herself. "I am helping Mr. Rowley here with his charm, so please do not think anything of our exchange as anything to gossip about."

"Oh, my lady, I would never—"

"Of course. But just in case," Percy said, knowing that as loyal as her maid was to her, if she thought that Percy had serious interest in Noah, it would be running through the house quicker than a mouse in mid-winter.

"Ah, here comes James as well."

"James?" Noah repeated.

"The valet."

"Right."

"James, this is Mr. Rowley," she said, introducing him to the servant, who bowed. "Mr. Rowley, James is prepared for you in one of the unused bedchambers."

Noah looked from the valet and back at her. "Where he is going to cut my hair?"

"Yes. James is very talented. Not to worry, I have ensured that you are in the best of hands."

She beamed at him with what she hoped he understood was encouragement before he sighed and left. Percy sat down to wait for him, pulling out the latest book of their club as she did so. She had to admit that while Hope's pick was rather sweet and cheerful, it was not nearly romantic enough for her liking.

She wondered how long James and Noah would take.

She couldn't wait to see what he looked like.

For the benefit of their ruse, of course. And nothing else.

* * *

NOAH STARED at himself in the vanity mirror in front of him as the servant stood behind him, his tools laid out before him. Was his appearance truly so contrary that he required such a drastic change?

"Mr. Rowley," the valet said politely, "before I begin, do you have a preference in what I do? Lady Percy has provided some direction, however, I would prefer to have your permission—"

Noah waved his hand in the air. "Whatever she said is fine."

"Very well. If you would like me to change anything as I proceed, please do say."

Noah nodded as the valet began. He was slow yet meticulous, and Noah began to ease slightly into the chair, no longer quite as concerned that the man might butcher him or, worse yet, be unsure of his way with the blade and cause irreversible damage. If Percy said he was the best, he would have to trust that he was the best.

"Would it be possible to remove your spectacles?"

Noah nodded, even though it meant that now he was truly giving all of his trust to the man, for everything past his nose was obscured.

"Very well," he said setting them down. "Go ahead now. Tell me when I can return them. Did you know the first wearable glasses came into being in Italy in the 13th century? Glass blowers made lenses of different thicknesses for wearers to try. It would be another four centuries, however, until an extension was added over the ears."

He looked up, sensing James staring at him as he remained motionless, holding a razor in his hand. Noah realized he wasn't sure how to respond.

"As you were," Noah said.

About an hour later, James stepped back away from him. "I believe I am finished now, my lord."

Noah reached out, finding his spectacles and sliding them on his nose, blinking as he stared at himself in the mirror. He recognized his face, but even it appeared altered with the change in his style. He tilted his head, studying himself.

"Is it satisfactory?" the valet asked.

"Yes," Noah said, nodding, for it was. He couldn't say exactly why, but it was a good change. The valet had reduced his sideburns and modernized the style of his hair on top so that it was longer over his forehead compared to the sides, which were cut shorter. The small bit of facial hair he had worn for years now was gone, and he rubbed his hand over his clean-shaven chin.

"Thank you, James," he finally said. "You did well."

"Of course," the man said as he tidied his tools and Noah eased himself out of the chair and walked toward the staircase, back to where Percy would be waiting. His stomach did an odd dip and roll, as he worried over what she might think when she saw him, how she would react... and why her opinion mattered so much to him.

He found her in the parlor still, her feet tucked up beneath her lap where she perched on the settee, her head in one hand, a book in the other. He paused, enjoying the scene before him, committing it to his memory like a painting he would carry around in his head.

Suddenly, she looked up as though she had sensed what he was doing.

A smile began to curl on her face, but then when she had her first good look at him, it stopped, fading.

She blinked, and then blinked again, her lips slightly open, her eyes wide. Noah waited for her to say something, but the longer she sat there, the more nervous he became.

Finally, he couldn't take it any longer.

"Well?" he said. "What do you think?"

* * *

PERCY KNEW she should say something.

Anything.

But she was too shocked to speak.

It was not as though Noah had drastically changed. And yet... there was a new awareness when she looked at him that made her stop and consider him in a different light than she ever had before.

She cleared her throat, sensing how uncomfortable she was making him by saying nothing. "You look... very nice."

Nice? That was the best she could do? He didn't comment on it, however, but simply nodded his head.

"Thank you. You were correct. James is very skilled."

Percy couldn't shake the odd sensation that had come over her as she looked at him, so she did what she always did and began to talk to ease her discomfort. She sensed Mary watching her from the corner of the room and remembered that she must act as normal as possible to ensure there was no gossip among the servants regarding her and Noah.

"Well. Now that the first part is done, it is time to continue, is it not? We should practice. I am quite delighted about this as I think you will be an excellent student. Not that there was any question about it. I am sure you excel at everything you do. I—yes. Anyway. We should begin."

"What are we practicing?" he asked, raising a brow.

"Flirting," she said, laughing at his startled expression. "I think we need a drink for this," she said, walking over to the sideboard, and pouring him dark amber liquid from a decanter into a short glass. He took a sip, watching closely as she did the same.

"Brandy?" he said, although instead of appearing shocked, he shook his head. "Somehow I am not surprised." He chuckled.

"Why, Noah, I believe you have some humor within you

after all," she said, then lifted a finger in the air. "That's good. We can work with that."

"I—"

"Oh, and please don't tell anyone about the brandy," she said, checking that no one had come near the door. "Same with you, Mary. I know it is not the most scandalous act possible, but I'd rather not have to explain myself."

"Understood," Noah said as Mary merely returned her attention to the sock she was darning.

Noah's frown had deepened, although why, Percy had no idea.

"Are you ready to begin?"

"Do I have a choice?"

"Of course. You always have a choice," she said, although she continued regardless. "Now. Pretend we are at this… club. I am the woman in question. You must come to speak to me. What do you say?"

He looked at her warily.

"I suppose it is always best to start with good evening."

CHAPTER 9

Noah no longer had any wish to do this. Everything within him was telling him to turn around and walk right out that parlor door. He knew how terrible he was at speaking to women. He didn't need Percy to realize it as well.

But he had made a promise. To Ashford, to Ashford's sister, and, most importantly, to Percy.

"Pretend I am her," Percy said, placing a hand on her hip, and he wanted to tell her that she could never be Mrs. MacNall, that she would always be perfectly Percy.

But he couldn't actually say that to her for she would read far too much into it.

"Good evening," he said instead. "It is good to see you."

She tilted her head and studied him. "That's fine," she said, "but that is not flirting. That is greeting my mother at a society event."

"I am doing my best," he said, trying not to show his impatience.

"Try this," she said. "Say the same thing, but with more emphasis on how *good* it is to see me. Lean in toward me.

THE SCHOLAR'S KEY

Then say it. Show me your interest. Run your hand down my arm. A little touch can go a long way."

"Very well," he said. "From the beginning?"

"Yes."

He stepped back and then forward again.

"Good evening," he repeated himself, but this time, he lifted his hand, settling in on Percy's arm, just above her elbow. He felt ridiculous, but she didn't seem upset at all.

He lowered his voice. "It is so good to see you." He ran his hand lightly down her arm, allowing it to fall just when his fingers brushed against hers. He kept his eyes locked on hers, knowing that he would never be able to do this with another – only with her.

"I am so happy you are here," she said, and he wondered if he caught a bit of breathlessness in her voice. "Did you come for me?"

"Yes."

She raised a brow.

"I came for enjoyment," he said. "For pleasure. So yes."

He watched her pupils dilate, headiness overwhelming him that he was causing a reaction within her. Perhaps he wasn't so bad at this after all.

"I-I see," she said, and Noah was strangely proud that he had caused her to become so disconcerted. "Is this your first time here?"

"It is," he said with a smile that was now easier to infuse with confidence. He wasn't sure if that was due to the brandy or her reaction. "You must be special, for I came here for you."

He leaned in again, placing his hand on the wall behind her, a stance that should have been unnatural to him but seemed to come easier with Percy before him. He was close enough that he could see the tiny freckles that dotted her nose, and he had to resist the strange urge to reach out and trace them.

"What particular interest do you have with me?" she asked, nearly breathless now.

"I was thinking," he murmured in a low voice, "that perhaps we could go somewhere more private. More comfortable."

A throat cleared from across the room, and Percy jumped, apparently having forgotten as much as Noah had that her maid was present. Which of course she was. Percy was a young woman with a reputation to uphold.

He stepped backward, returning his hand to himself.

"So?" he said, adjusting his spectacles, trying to compose himself. "Do you think that will do?"

"I believe it will, yes," she said, nodding furiously, for once, it seemed, at something of a loss for words. "Then you will go from the club to Mrs. MacNall's home and try to find the jewellery?"

"I suppose," he said. "Unless she is wearing them. That would be ideal."

"Likely not at such a place," Percy said rather forlornly. "Then—"

"Persephone?"

"Oh!" Percy said, her hand coming to her mouth. "That will be my mother. Before she enters, tell me, did you have a chance to speak to Lord Chesterham?"

"Briefly. He knew nothing about rubies."

She nodded, frowning. "Must have been given to her by another. Here she comes."

As if on cue, Lady Fairfax entered the parlor, eyebrows rising in interest when she noted Noah's presence.

"Mr. Rowley," she said. "How are you? This is an unexpected visit."

THE SCHOLAR'S KEY

Noah bowed toward her. "Yes. My apologies, Lady Fairfax, I did not know that you would be out."

A small noise from the corner reached his ear, one that sounded something like a skeptical cough from Mary.

"When I discovered Lady Percy was in Bath, I came to pay my regards and update her on the status of our mutual acquaintances. I should, however, be going."

"It is lovely to see you," Lady Fairfax murmured as Percy followed him to the door of the parlor.

"I will be in touch, Mr. Rowley," Percy said, and as much as he wished that was the case, he was well aware that there was nothing further for them to do together, as much as he yearned to see her again.

For even if he must change his hair, his wardrobe, and his demeanor, if it meant spending time with Percy, well, he was willing to do it.

* * *

PERCY HAD no idea if she was doing the right thing the next day. She knew she should just let the situation be. She had done more than was required of her regarding Noah and his mission with Mrs. MacNall. But they had not discussed what he was going to do once he arrived, which bothered her more than she would like to admit. Would he follow through and have relations with her?

The thought made Percy sick to her stomach.

Only because she would never want to see him being used in such a way.

At least, that was what she told herself.

However, she still found herself standing in the foyer of the home where she knew he was working the next day, wondering just how she was going to secure an audience with him without raising any suspicion. He had told her he was studying in the Worthington library, and she hoped her visit was acceptable.

"May I be of any assistance?" a butler asked, and she looked back and forth for Noah but saw no sign of him.

"I am looking for Mr. Noah Rowley," she said. "The historian," she added when the butler's face remained blank.

"I will go ask him to come meet you," the servant said, but Percy held out a hand to stop him.

"Would it be possible for me to meet with him in the library?"

The butler hesitated.

"He is my husband," Percy said with her most winning smile, which seemed to be enough to convince him.

"Of course. Follow me."

Percy, with Mary at her heels, followed the man up the stairs and down a corridor until they stopped in front of ornate library doors.

"Mr. Rowley?" the butler called as he knocked on the door. "You have a visitor." No response emerged, and when he opened the door, Noah was sitting with his head down over the desk, his finger sliding down the page of the book in front of him as his lips moved, talking to himself.

"Mr. Rowley?" the butler repeated, clearing his throat, and finally Noah looked up, blinking a few times.

Percy stood still in the doorway, glad someone else was between them and she didn't have to speak yet. For the same awareness that had overcome her at the house yesterday began to creep over her again as she took him in, with his hair styled in a new way and a jacket that, while likely still his old one, seemed to have been altered slightly. Perhaps the tailor had made some suggestions for Noah's current wardrobe.

But it was not just his appearance that had suddenly captured her attention. Watching him work, she appreciated his intelligence, his drive to do something more than squander his family's wealth and connections for meaningless pleasure as many second sons did. He could be witty when he liked, but most often he never spoke unless he had something consequential to say.

So unlike herself.

"Lady Percy," he said, standing, a slight flare of his nostrils telling her that he was surprised to see her. "What brings you here?"

"I was hoping to speak to you privately," she said, and he nodded.

"Of course. Thank you, Sampson," he said to the butler, before gesturing to a seat in front of the desk. "Mary, would you like to sit?" he asked her maid, gesturing to a corner chair, surprising Percy, for no one ever spoke to her maid.

"Actually, Mary," she murmured as she turned, "would you mind waiting in the corridor?"

"Of course, my lady," Mary said, although Percy didn't miss her suspicious glance toward Noah. Apparently, her privacy would be at the expense of gossip.

When the door shut behind her, it seemed as though all of the air was sucked out with it, as suddenly Percy, who spoke far more than anyone ever should, was bereft of anything to say.

"Please, sit," Noah said again, and Percy did, pleased when he took the chair beside hers instead of the one across the desk.

"How long have you been here at this home?" she asked, actually interested in learning more about his work.

"A few days here," he said. "Always the mornings and usually the afternoons as well, although I make exceptions now and again."

"Like yesterday?" she asked, annoyed by the flicker of

pleasure that licked at her at the thought that he had seen visiting her important enough to break his work.

"Yes," he confirmed.

"When are you visiting the Queen's Hand?" she asked.

"Likely tonight," he said, shifting back and forth in his chair, signalling that he was not, perhaps, as eager to take on this role as he tried to make out that he was.

"Do you feel that you are prepared?" she asked, secretly hoping that he would tell her that he was, thanks to her efforts yesterday.

"I hope so," was all he said, as he tapped a finger against his lips.

"Aha," she said, lifting a finger. "That is where you go wrong."

"I am not prepared?"

"No, you must not *hope* that you are prepared. You say that you *are* prepared. You must be confident."

"Very well. I am prepared."

"That lacked conviction."

He rubbed his brow. "I am doing the best that I can."

She noted his exasperation, and sat back, slightly subdued now. "I know. I do apologize."

"So what brings you here?" he asked, leaning back in his chair, although she noticed that their knees were not far apart from where they sat side by side.

It was a good question. What had brought her here? She wasn't sure that she could rightly answer that. She had been agitated when she considered all that he would encounter at the nightclub.

"What do you intend to do with Mrs. MacNall?"

"Pardon me?"

"If you return to her home... what will you do with her?"

He folded his arms across his chest, and she thought she just might detect the slightest of smirks growing on his face.

"Why, Percy, do you care what I do?"

"Of course," she said. "I would not like you to compromise your... integrity."

"How do you know that I have integrity?"

"I just do. You are a gentleman, if there ever was one."

Which was true. If there was ever a man she would say she trusted to do the right thing, it was he.

He leaned forward. "Lady Percy. Do not concern yourself with what I will or will not do with Mrs. MacNall. The most important thing is that I succeed in finding the necklace, is it not?"

"I suppose."

Except it wasn't. It wasn't at all.

"Well, there is one more thing that you might need to learn," she said, uncertain why she was grasping for a reason to stay.

"Which is?"

"The art of seduction."

CHAPTER 10

The art of seduction?

Noah lifted his brow. "I am interested to know why you feel that you should be the one to teach me," he said. He had always assumed that she was an innocent young woman, but was he, perhaps, wrong in his assumption? He supposed there was only one way to find out. "Flirting, perhaps, but seduction? Is that a topic you are skilled in, Percy?"

Her cheeks began to flush, the pink rising from her neck up to her defined cheekbones most becomingly.

"I-I am not, exactly, *accomplished* in the matter, but I have read a great many books. And I thought I could help. Who else can you speak to about this?"

"Are you assuming that I do not know how to seduce a woman?"

"I never said that. I—"

"It's all right," he said, taking pity on her. "I wouldn't blame you if you did. But I assure you, I shall be just fine."

He also had no wish to discuss this any further with her, lest she find out his true inexperience with the subject. It wasn't that he had never been with a woman before — it had just not been particularly often.

"I find it quite interesting to study the most renowned of seducers," he said instead, changing the subject. "Casanova, Cleopatra… Lord Byron."

"You are going to seduce Mrs. MacNall, then?"

"Does it matter to you?"

Her jaw snapped shut at that, and she looked away from him. He had to tamp down the small glow in his chest that she apparently did not want to see him with another woman.

"I do not want to see your name associated with a mistress who is connected to another man," she said.

"I see," he said. "So you are concerned for me, then."

She let out a sigh as she began to stand, but he reached out and placed a hand on her arm. "My apologies. I was only teasing, but perhaps I am not so proficient at that, either. I would like you to stay. Please."

"Very well," she said warily. "Let me see it then."

"See what?"

"This seduction that you are so proficient at."

"Oh," he said, sitting back now. He hadn't thought that he would be expected to perform, here in this library in the middle of the day. But if he didn't, he was sure she would assume his ineptitude.

He took a breath. He could do this, just as he had flirted with her at her house. He just had to pretend that he was someone else – someone like his brother. Take on that personality.

And, with Percy, it wasn't just a game. All he had to do was speak the truth, even if she thought that he was only acting.

He shifted forward so that he was sitting on the edge of the chair, touching his knees against hers.

"We are alone."

"We are."

"I believe we need some entertainment."

"Such as?"

"Entertainment that we can create ourselves," he said, leaning forward and brushing a loose tendril of hair back behind her ear.

Her eyes widened and her nostrils flared with a swift intake of breath, but she sat straight up in front of him.

"I shall have you know, my lord, that I am paid very well by a generous man to be loyal to him and only him."

"What will it hurt if he never finds out?"

"You are very sure of yourself."

"I have no reason not to be," he said with a smile, even though this was belying all his true insecurities. Despite feeling an imposter, he was encouraged by her reaction to him. "What your protector doesn't know won't hurt him. I shall be your secret, and you shall be mine."

"With a proposal like that, how could I refuse?" she said, her lips widening slightly. "But do tell me, my lord... why are you worth the risk?"

Noah's heart was beating hard and fast now, and as much as he continued to tell himself that this was all a game, practice for their true purpose, he was having difficulty remembering it. A large part of him wanted to believe that she felt the same. How could she not, with that flush in her cheeks, the rapid rise and fall of her chest as her aquamarine eyes stared into his?

"Because," he said, licking his lips, "I will take you places that no other man has ever taken you before."

Her eyes blinked rapidly at that, and her lips parted as she remained still before him. He leaned in, knowing that this was the time in the seduction when he would take action. This was just supposed to be practice, and yet when she looked at him like that...

She closed the gap between them, and his body moved before he could think. Her hands reached out, grabbing his shoulders while his arms wrapped around her back, pulling her in tight toward him. While their lips pressed against one another with an urgency he only ever could have imagined, the soft curves of her breasts squeezed against his chest. When the tip of her tongue flicked against his lips, he couldn't deny opening them to her, inviting her in while his tongue moved against hers.

They were sitting somewhat awkwardly, and while Noah wanted to lift her and place her down on his lap, he was too scared to do so, for if he did, it might break this spell they were caught in. She would come to her senses, let him go—and then this wondrous occasion would end, and she would likely refuse to ever see him again, let alone engage in any further time spent alone.

She moaned slightly as her fingers slid through his hair, holding his head against her, and he realized that, shockingly, she wanted this just as much as he did.

His gasp of delight seemed to be enough to wake her, as she stilled and slowly drew away from him.

It was not the horror he had assumed would cover her face, but she did appear to be surprised, at the very least.

"Noah... I-I'm sorry."

"Sorry?" he blinked as he adjusted his spectacles, which had become rather askew. "Whatever for?"

Her fingertips were pressing against her lips, and he wished he was the one still upon them.

"For my forwardness." She stood now, backing up slowly toward the door, and he reached out a hand when she slightly stumbled. "I am so sorry. I allowed that to go too far, believing... well. It doesn't matter what I believe. Suffice it to say, you were correct. You do not appear to need any advice. Or practice."

She backed up until she bumped into the door, and she jumped in surprise.

"Oh goodness," she said, and Noah couldn't help but smile that she was as flustered as he was. He waited, knowing that when she was flustered, she was likely to keep talking. And, given how much he enjoyed listening to her, he didn't stop her. "I wonder what Mary must think. She is loyal, but I do know she loves to gossip, as she is always telling me the latest in the servants' quarters. Which only leads me to wonder what she tells everyone about me. Although she has never provided any information to my mother that has returned to me. However, because of her, my mother will learn that I have come to visit you today. What business could have brought me to be with you in this library? I do not even know the family who lives here, for goodness' sake. Perhaps... well..."

She tapped her finger against her lips.

"Perhaps you could tell her that you were inviting me and my aunt and uncle to dinner," he said, the idea out of his mouth before he had time to fully consider it. For if that is what she told them, then they were sure to actually invite him to dinner. This would mean another engagement with Percy, except this would be one in which she would be sitting across from him, so close yet so out of reach, with no opportunity to touch her, to spend time alone with her.

Although that was likely done with as well.

"I like that idea!" She beamed, but then her smile fell quickly. "That is — if you want to see me again. You must think me a wanton. I assure you, Noah, that I do not actually have any real experience in the art of seduction, truly. I—"

As she spoke, she stepped away from the door and began walking toward him again. He stood, placing his hand over hers where it now rested on her chair.

"Percy. I understand. You do not need to feel any shame over that. I—I enjoyed it."

"You did?" Her eyes widened. "Not that I didn't. For I did. It's just, I don't know what came over me. One moment we were acting – practicing – and the next…"

She had been overwhelmed by the roles they were playing. Right. It was not that she had any interest in him, any desire to kiss him. She had been caught up in the moment. She did not feel as he did, and he'd best remember that before he got too far ahead of himself.

"You played your part well," he said, trying to soften the terseness in his voice with a small smile, but he was worried it appeared more like a grimace. "I never would have believed that you were not a woman who was interested in… more."

"Right," she said with a quick nod. "Well. This was an… elucidating afternoon."

Elucidating?

"I best be going, however," she continued. "Mary will have so many questions. Although she would never voice them aloud. Of course."

She lifted a hand to her mouth again, almost as though she was trying to force herself to stop talking.

"Good afternoon, Noah."

And with that, she fled in a flurry of pink skirts and cherry blossoms.

Leaving him overwhelmed with arousal and interest in her wake.

CHAPTER 11

*P*ercy was mortified. She had kissed – kissed! – Noah Rowley.

That was not just a kiss but a full-on attack. What must he think of her? He had said that he was fine with it, but there they had been, practicing his upcoming encounter with Mrs. MacNall, and she couldn't have said what came over her. As they had spoken, she had drawn closer toward him until suddenly the tension that had been pulling them together snapped and she'd placed her lips on his.

It was her first real kiss, besides the odd quick kiss that she had stolen in her first season.

If someone had asked her a month ago if she could ever imagine herself kissing Noah Rowley, she likely would have laughed. He was quiet and bookish, the last man she ever would have thought would come forward and show any interest in her.

But when they began their practice – for she could hardly pretend she was teaching him as the man clearly knew what he was doing, even more than she did – he had turned into another person entirely, and shown her what could be possible.

That was the problem with Percy. She made the possible reality. She had always enjoyed pretending to be someone else. As a child, she had set up shows with her dolls and entertained her governess and her brother by acting out scenes she had created herself.

She had mostly rid herself of those notions as she had grown up, aware that there was no outlet for her interest, but this time with Noah had allowed her to pretend to be someone else again.

What she couldn't decide was whether the kiss had been through the guise of the role she was playing, or through her own emotion.

It was rather disconcerting.

She had just entered the home they were renting, Mary close behind her. She hadn't asked Percy anything, thank goodness, and Percy had been trying to ignore the curious glances that her maid sent her way.

Emotions were swirling within the pit of her stomach, and she was having a hard time coming to terms with just exactly what they were.

It was expected, yes, after such out-of-character actions, but there was something more there. Something akin to… annoyance. Or anger.

But why?

"Persephone?"

She looked up to find her mother standing in the arch leading to the drawing room.

"Yes?"

"I hadn't realized you had gone out," she said, not one to be outright inquisitive, but clearly curious as to where Percy had been. Knowing that it would likely get back to her mother through the servants, anyway, Percy decided the best thing to do was to be honest – to an extent.

"I went to visit a friend," she said, hoping her mother wouldn't ask any further questions.

"Oh?"

"I went to see how Mr. Rowley was getting on. He doesn't know anyone in Bath besides his family, and he does not make friends easily."

"I see. That is… kind of you."

"Yes, well I promised Lord Ashford and Cassandra that I would check in on him, and I told him that we would invite him, along with his aunt and uncle, to dinner. If that is all right with you?"

Her mother's eyebrows rose, but she didn't comment besides to say, "Of course. Shall we make it tomorrow?"

Tomorrow. After he visited Mrs. MacNall's club. She supposed she should want to know if he was successful in his quest to find the necklace but wasn't certain that she wanted to know the rest of it.

Which, she realized, was where the source of her anger came from. She was annoyed that he was now taking all they had developed together and was going to use it with another woman.

But there was nothing she could do about it.

Except wait and question herself as to just why she cared so much.

* * *

Noah hadn't even been able to enjoy dinner with his aunt and uncle, so worried was he about the evening to come. There were so many potential downfalls. He could fail to interest Mrs. MacNall, fail to be invited back to her house, fail to find the necklace, fail to leave with it.

Of course, the actions necessary for each step terrified him just as much as any other, but at least he wouldn't have any witnesses. Namely, Percy.

He stood in front of the Queen's Hand, shifting back and forth from one foot to the other. He had never been the type of man to frequent such establishments, but only someone who knew him would question his presence there.

He took a breath of courage and pushed open the door, immediately overwhelmed by the smoke and darkness that washed over him. He paused for a moment, allowing his eyes to adjust to the light, before slowly shuffling inside. He received a few cursory looks, but no one seemed particularly interested in him or what he was doing there.

Most of the patrons seemed of a similar ilk to him – wealthy enough to afford the latest fashions, and, likely, at least a night with one of the women who decorated the room. This was no low-class brothel, for the women were dressed in fabrics as fine as those worn by any lady of the *ton*, only these gowns were richer, more vibrant, and required much less imagination as to just what was hidden underneath.

He spotted Mrs. MacNall across the room, her dark hair artfully arranged beneath an exquisite hat that he knew would not have been cheaply made. He was too far away to determine whether or not she wore the necklace, but he began to weave his way across the room toward her. The sooner he accomplished his goal here, the better.

"Well, you are a fresh face."

He hadn't progressed far when another woman stepped into his path. Her hair was dark, reminding him of Percy, except that he did not react to this woman, whereas when he thought of Percy, his feelings went in all kinds of directions – none of which he was particularly happy about.

"I am new to Bath," he said, stepping to the side to try to avoid the woman, but she was not to be deterred.

"Then you must be interested in making new friends," she practically purred.

"I have quite a few friends already, as it happens," he said, "although I thank you for your interest."

He couldn't help but be polite, for it was not this woman's fault for assuming that he might be interested in something more than a few passing comments.

She smiled tersely but allowed him to continue, and he kept his head down as he began to walk toward the back of the room and Mrs. MacNall.

He stopped, however, when another familiar face caught his eye. Lord Stephen. He knew he should keep walking, that wasting time with him would not help this situation, but ire began to build in him. So this man was pursuing Percy and yet had no issue in frequenting such an establishment and paying beautiful women to fall over his lap. He knew that it was a common occurrence, that it should have no bearing upon him, and yet, he couldn't help the frustration that washed over him when he considered that this man was lucky enough to have an opportunity with such a woman and yet was willing to risk squandering it.

For if he knew Percy – and he liked to think that he was becoming more familiar with her – she would not take kindly to such actions if she learned of them. Although, she had not appeared to be particularly pleased with him the other night either.

"Lord Stephen," he grunted, standing over the man as he smoked a cheroot in one hand and fondled a woman's bosom with the other. "I would not have expected to see you here."

"Mr. Rowan, is it?" Lord Stephen said lazily, a gleam in his eye telling Noah that he knew exactly what his true name was.

"Rowley," he said through gritted teeth.

"That's right. Mutual acquaintance and all that? You know Lady Percy, do you not?"

"I do."

"I'll be sure you are invited to the wedding."

He threw back his head and laughed at that, as though aware of exactly what Noah felt for Percy.

"Does your *betrothed* know you are here?" Noah asked, drawing out the word to make it clear that he knew perfectly well that no promises had yet been made.

"It's no business of hers what I do with my time," he said with a shrug. "Besides, you have a penchant for her yourself, do you not, Mr. Rowley? To share my sin would be to admit yours."

He grinned then, and Noah could only smile tersely and continue walking. He wasn't about to share with Lord Stephen that not only was Percy well aware that he was here, but she had, in fact, encouraged him to come. It was too bad he couldn't tell him, for he would have loved to have seen the look on his face at such information.

He was surprised to find, when he looked up, that Mrs. MacNall was watching him, through eyes hooded and lowered.

"Mr. Rowley," she drawled. "I never imagined you would show here."

"You underestimate me," he said, drawing close to her, leaning a hip against the wooden column beside her. "I am far from what most expect of me."

"I see that," she said, tilting her head as she studied him. "You look... different."

He forced his lips up into a small smile. He knew how his hairstyle had changed his appearance, and how much better the cut of his jacket and trousers fit him. But, strangely, his acting out the situation with Percy had most aided him, giving him a confidence that he hadn't possessed before. If he had caused Percy to experience arousal at his attempted seduction, then there was a chance he could achieve his aim with Mrs. MacNall.

"Perhaps it is due to your company," he said now, hoping his tone was flirtatious, although truthfully, he had no idea how it sounded.

She smiled, although she seemed suspicious.

"Are you a charmer, then, Mr. Rowley?"

"I try to be," he said, although the words, which had come so easy with Percy, seemed to stick in his throat.

He looked down for her necklace but found her neck, unfortunately, bare. Of course, it wouldn't be that easy. When he looked up, he found her watching him with a smirk, and he realized that she had misread just where his gaze had been directed.

Not that he had missed her ample, burgeoning bosom. That would be nearly impossible.

He just hadn't been greatly intrigued by it, was all.

"Shall we sit?" she asked, gesturing toward one of the chesterfields that had been laid haphazardly around the room.

"Of course," he said, taking a seat, stiffening when she sat so close to him that her arm was resting upon his. Unlike Percy's touch, hers had quite the opposite effect, and he wanted nothing more than to stand and walk away.

But of course, that would not help him achieve his purpose.

"Tell me of this... protector of yours," Noah said. "Is he a jealous man?"

Mrs. MacNall laughed, a fake, tinkling laugh, so unlike Percy's deep and honest one.

"I suppose you could say that," she said. "But he does not own me."

"He just pays for you to live," Noah said before he could stop himself, and she raised an eyebrow.

"Do you judge me for that, Mr. Rowley?"

"Not at all," he said truthfully. "I am simply trying to better understand the situation."

"Very well, then," she said, her lips curling into a smile. "Buy me a drink?"

He nodded, doing as she asked. He flirted with her as best he could, slightly annoyed when Lord Stephen began to walk toward them, his resolve clear. He intended to pursue Mrs. MacNall for himself. Which Noah had no problem with – except that he needed to be the one to go home with her tonight.

"Mrs. MacNall," he said, leaning in close. "Perhaps we could go somewhere more private?"

"You do not enjoy an audience?" she said with a laugh.

"I do not."

"Very well," she said with a shrug. "There are back rooms."

Oh, dear. He needed access to her house.

"As it happens, I do not wish anyone to know of my actions here," he said.

"We are discreet."

"Be that as it may... I am courting a young woman and cannot have her aware of any other... encounters I may have."

She paused for a moment in contemplation.

"Very well," she said. "My house is not far. We can take our evening there."

"Very good," he said, although inside he was in turmoil.

For as pleased as he was that he would have the opportunity to look for the necklace, there was just one other problem – what Mrs. MacNall would expect him to do when he arrived.

CHAPTER 12

Noah followed the woman into the house, unsure of what he had assumed but appreciative of the home within. Mrs. MacNall had rather exacting tastes, it appeared, and he couldn't help but think that Percy would approve of the jewel tones that decorated the room, from the paper on the walls to the furniture to the sculptures and paintings that were obviously quite valuable.

"Your home is very fine indeed," he said, not missing her smile at his comment.

"Thank you," she said. "I am quite proud of it."

Seeing his opportunity, he continued. "You are obviously a woman who appreciates fine things."

"I do."

"The last time I saw you, you were wearing a necklace that was most exquisite."

"My rubies," she said, her eyes turning on him sharply. "They received quite a bit of attention."

"I can see why," he said, hoping his words appeared calm and collected, even while his inward thoughts were muddled. "They must be very valuable. Did you buy them yourself?"

"I did not," she said. "They were a gift."

"From your protector."

"Actually," she said, "they were from another."

"I see," he said. "I apologize for my questions. It is simply that the woman I am courting also appreciates rubies and I know how much she would love such a piece of jewellery. I was hoping to buy her a similar piece."

Mrs. MacNall sat back in her chair, resting her head on one hand as she stared at him. "She is a lucky woman. I received them from a... friend, but unfortunately, I cannot give his name. As I said, I am discreet. But he told me he bought it from a shop that specializes in such items."

Noah had a feeling it was a shop of stolen goods, but he wasn't about to say so.

"Would it be possible for me to see it again?" he asked. "The woman I am courting, she saw it as well, and she was quite interested."

"She wouldn't happen to be Lady Persephone Holloway, now would she?"

"Ah—y-yes, she is," he said, realizing that he had walked himself into a lie. He only hoped that when Mrs. MacNall said she practiced discretion, she meant in all matters. For he wasn't sure how Percy would accept a rumor that the two of them were near to betrothed.

Mrs. MacNall studied him for a moment before she walked down a corridor, turning through a door that must be her bedroom. Noah closed his eyes and listened, hearing the jingle of a key and then the click of a drawer. So she must have it locked away somewhere. She emerged moments later, the gold and red jewellery draped over her fingers.

"Here you are," she said, and he lifted it, studying it as though he was appreciating its beauty, but the truth was, he was looking for where the key could possibly fit. He wished he had more time to thoroughly examine it, but she was already reaching for it and he reluctantly returned it. "It's beautiful," he said, just as he caught sight of the ruby heart in the middle of the lock – and what appeared to be a hole in the gold plate behind it.

"Thank you," she said, before taking it and walking it back to the room. He followed her, hoping he could make her believe that he was interested in what he could do for her there.

He stood in the doorway, leaning against the frame, attempting to appear nonchalant, but he watched her as closely as possible, seeing where she unlocked the drawer and then replaced the necklace. She turned the key before tucking it away in a bag that she then hid in the depths of the wardrobe. She hadn't seen him yet, and he turned away, looking outward to the corridor, until he heard her step closer behind him.

"Now," she said, wrapping a hand around his neck, "what comes next?"

Noah closed his eyes and took a breath. He knew that most men in his position would go along with this willingly, but the truth was, he had such little desire to follow through with her, for all he could think about was how untrue that would be to Percy – whether or not Percy herself had any care for his loyalty or would ever actually return his affections.

But how was he going to get out of this?

Finally, he decided that, like in most situations in life, the best solution was to tell the truth.

He turned around, taking a step backward so that she wasn't touching him anymore.

"Mrs. MacNall—"

"Marianne."

"Marianne. I don't know how to say this, for you seem a

lovely woman and I thought I was interested, truly I did, but I find my thoughts are rather preoccupied with the young woman I previously mentioned."

"Lady Persephone."

"Yes."

She stared at him for a beat.

"Then why, might I ask, did you go to such trouble to seek me out, to return to my home? Was there something else that you were looking for?"

Did she suspect his true aim?

"Experience, Mrs. MacNall. I was looking for experience. But I find that my body is not complying with what I came searching for."

"I see," she said, although he could tell that she held her suspicions. "Well, then, Mr. Rowley, perhaps our paths will cross again. I hope that you receive all that you wish from your Lady Persephone."

He nodded his head, pausing in the doorway, realizing that she likely expected something more from him.

"Is this enough?" he asked, holding out two guineas, but she shook her head with a smile.

"I did nothing," she said.

"But for your time," he insisted, but she reached out, closing his fingers back around the coins.

"You are a gentleman, Mr. Rowley, which is a rarity these days. Thank you for showing me that men like you still exist. Now, good luck with your young woman."

She stood on her toes, pressing a quick kiss against his cheek before opening the door and showing him out.

Suddenly he was feeling quite regretful – for while he had no romantic notions toward Mrs. MacNall, he found he rather liked her – which was going to make stealing from her all the more distasteful.

***

Percy was trying to be patient.

But the time between when she and Noah had last spoken – and kissed – and the dinner with Noah and his aunt and uncle seemed to take a sennight, even though it was truly only a day.

She would like to say it was because she wondered whether or not he had found the necklace, and if he had, what secrets the necklace had imparted.

But she found that what was mostly on her mind was what exactly Noah had done to achieve his aim.

It irked her that she cared, and she wondered why it so bothered her. She supposed the only explanation was guilt for being part of the reason why he might go against his morals.

For there was no other reasonable explanation.

There was a quick knock on her door before her mother opened it slightly and smiled through the crack.

"Percy, time to go downstairs. Our guests will be arriving soon. The family is already here waiting."

"Of course," Percy said, smiling at Mary in the mirror as she took one final look at herself. She had worn one of her favorites, a lilac dress that was cut demurely but flattered her bosom as well as her collarbones and shoulders. Her maid had done as wonderful a job on her hair as she always did, pinning it up loosely enough that it hung softly, the darkness of her hair accented by the small gold diamond earrings hanging from her lobes.

Now her heart was beating in anticipation as she wondered just how she would capture Noah alone.

"Is everything all right, darling?" her mother asked as they descended the stairs.

"Perfectly fine, of course," Percy said, forcing a confident smile on her face. What was wrong with her? Why, she was acting like Mr. Rowley himself at the moment. "I look forward to this evening."

"As do I," her mother said, patting her hand. "I think it will be most... illuminating."

"Why would you say that?" Percy asked, frowning at her. "I thought in addition to Mr. Rowley and his aunt and uncle it was only Aunt Hannah attending with Rebecca and Elizabeth."

"They are here yes. But... do not be angry with me," her mother said, her eyes pleading with her. "I never meant for this, truly I didn't. It is only that today I was in the park with Lady—"

"Lady Fairfax!" a voice rang out.

Percy caught herself just in time before she groaned aloud. She had asked her mother not to do this again, and yet here she was, with her unwelcome surprise yet again.

"Lady Lecher. Lord Stephen," Percy said, forcing a smile on her face when her mother elbowed her lightly in the ribs as she originally said nothing. She caught her cousins standing behind them, knowing grins on their faces. "It is... surprising to see you."

"I was so pleased when your mother invited us," Lady Lecher said. "Although I must admit, when I heard you were having company this evening, I invited myself, so I cannot be too thankful, now, can I?"

She laughed, and Percy's mother turned to Percy with a shrug of her shoulders as though to say, "See, it was out of my control," but Percy believed that one always had the option to say no.

"My dear Lady Persephone," Lord Stephen said, picking up her hand, but Percy snatched it back before he could place his lips on the back of it. "It is lovely to see you again. I was hoping we would have the opportunity to spend more time together."

"Yes. Here we are," Percy said, not wanting to commit to anything.

"Now—"

But Percy couldn't have said what it was that Lord Stephen said next. For though he continued to speak, she lost all ability to pay any attention to his words. It was at that moment that the drawing room doors opened once more, revealing the butler with guests behind him. When he stepped in, announced them, and then moved out of the way, Percy couldn't help but be instantly drawn to the man standing within the door frame. He looked the same as he always did – medium stature, medium build, brown hair, brown eyes, spectacles. Thanks to her, the valet, and the tailor, however, there was an air about him now that captivated Percy, making it impossible for her to look away.

And he was gazing right back, as though they were the only two people in the room, two people who had been waiting for one another, whose time apart had been agony.

She finally realized that she was staring, her focus completely on the man who now stood alone in the threshold of the room, for his aunt and uncle had continued without him.

"Lady Percy," Lord Stephen said insistently from beside her. "I asked you something."

Another elbow entered her ribs, and she elbowed back. She was going to have bruises on her side.

"Yes," her cousin Rebecca hissed in her ear.

"Yes," she repeated, uncertain just what his question was.

"I may call on you to ride in my phaeton tomorrow?" he asked, smugness in his voice.

THE SCHOLAR'S KEY

Drat, that was not at all what she had wanted to agree to.

"A phaeton!" Rebecca said, her mouth agape, and Percy wondered just when her cousins had joined her. Did they not understand this was a private conversation?

"Oh, I love phaetons," Elizabeth said. "You will have such fun."

"You will," Rebecca said.

"Not tomorrow," Percy said hurriedly, trying to shush her cousins. "Perhaps next week."

Lord Stephen looked between the three of them before focusing his expression on Percy.

"If I didn't know better, I would say you were avoiding me."

She just lifted a brow as Elizabeth and Rebecca filled the silence for her, denying his words. Percy didn't argue, for that would cross the line, even for her, but the truth was, she didn't care what he thought.

For if he thought the truth was anything else, then he was either not particularly intelligent or so certain of himself that he would never suspect a young woman would not be interested in his courtship. Her gaze, however, was on another man, one who, right now, was farther from her than she would have liked.

Noah's gaze narrowed in on them, his expression troubled, likely when he saw not only that extra people had been invited, but that Lord Stephen was among them.

Percy had hoped to capture a few moments alone with him. How was she to do that now?

She took matters into her own hands and crossed the room, greeting him and his aunt, all politeness, although she hoped her stare upon him told him that she had much more to say. As they all made their greetings, Percy found that the awareness that she had noticed before showed no signs of dimming as she had hoped. Instead, it seemed that it was only growing. But why, oh why?

Percy finally found she couldn't deny it any longer.

She was attracted to Mr. Noah Rowley.

And she had no idea just what she was supposed to do about it.

CHAPTER 13

Noah could feel Percy watching him. He knew why – she wanted to know whether or not he had achieved his goal of finding the necklace. He waited through the drinks they shared in the drawing room before the dinner. He waited through the dinner itself, all of the five courses, each that were progressively more delicious. He waited through the after-dinner drinks the men took in the dining room while the women retired to the drawing room.

During dinner, he listened to Miss Elizabeth chattering away in his ear, and he nodded his head and made the appropriate "hmms" and "ahhs" when necessary.

After dinner, he watched Lord Stephen tell lecherous jokes, exchanging a glance with his uncle, who appeared to be equally annoyed by the crudeness with which the man spoke. Lord Fairfax, himself, did not appear to be particularly pleased, which made Noah wonder just why he thought the man might make a match for his daughter.

Perhaps he was starting to wonder if he had made the right decision.

They began their walk into the drawing room just as Percy was stepping out of it.

"Percy," her father rumbled. "We were just coming to join you."

"I will be but a moment," she said with a small smile as she entered the corridor.

Noah lingered just behind the other men as they walked into the drawing room, and she looked behind her as though sensing his pause. She glanced about from one side to the other before tilting her head toward another door and he followed after her, unable to do anything but answer her request.

"We do not have long," she said softly as she shut the door behind them after they entered the small parlor. She stepped closer to him, wringing her hands in front of her. "You must tell me what happened."

"I saw the necklace," he said, enticed by the cherry blossoms that seemed to envelop her. "She keeps it locked in a box in her wardrobe. The key was also in the wardrobe, in a small bag within its depths. I convinced her to show me the necklace, but I had only the opportunity to hold it for the briefest moment, not to examine it."

"How did you convince her?"

"I told her that I recalled the necklace from the night I had met her and that the woman I was courting was interested in rubies."

"Did she ask who you were courting?"

He paused. "She did." Goodness, was he going to have to tell her?

"Well, who did you say it was?" she demanded, and he sighed.

"She guessed it was you, and I confirmed her suspicion," he said, his face warming as he scratched his head, almost surprised when he didn't find the long hair on the side that had been there for so long. "I apologize, Percy. I never meant for you to become involved."

She laughed, although there were nerves within it. "I was just as involved as you from the start. Besides, I do not mind."

A flutter of hope burst through his chest. "You don't?"

"Not at all," she said. "If that is the little bit that I must do to help, then I am happy to do it."

"Very well," he said, relieved that she did not seem overly concerned. "I did ask that she not share the information, so hopefully you shall be protected."

She nodded as she shifted her weight from one foot to the other, and he guessed she was likely waiting for his ideas on the next steps.

"There is only one thing to do now," he said.

"What's that?"

"I must return and steal the necklace," he said resolutely, trying to convince himself as much as share the information with her. "Even though I would prefer not to, for I actually rather highly regard Mrs. MacNall."

"Y-you do?" Percy said, her eyes wide and worried, concerning him.

"Yes. She was understanding when I told her that I could not follow through with our... liaison."

A smile stretched across Percy's face, but it was gone so fast that Noah wondered whether he had been seeing things or not.

"You didn't go through with it?"

He shook his head, knowing that he shouldn't be speaking of such things with her, but she had asked, and somehow she needed to understand that he hadn't.

"No," he said. "I told her that... it would not be true to the woman I was courting."

"To... me?"

"Yes."

"I see," she breathed, stepping closer to him, and every nerve ending on his body seemed to light up at her closeness. "That is very loyal of you."

"I couldn't follow through," he said, his breath quickening. "It didn't seem right."

"Of course," she said, dipping her head, and Noah couldn't help but remember what her pillowy lips had felt like under his, as he longed to feel them once more.

"We should be getting back," he said as their heads neared, her breath as quick as his.

"We should."

"I am glad I had the chance to talk to you privately."

"As am I."

"Tell me the truth," she said, raising her face to his. "Why did you leave Mrs. MacNall's?"

"Because," he said, their lips only inches apart. He shouldn't tell her the truth. It would change everything between them, and they had so much more to do together. "I could not stop thinking about you."

That was when he dipped his head, closing the space between them, his lips moving over hers. It was everything he had remembered and more. Her hands reached up, her fingers clinging around the lapels of his jacket as she pulled him closer and his arms wrapped around her back, skimming over the soft fabric of her dress. He had wondered if she had been acting before, but there was no need for her to do so now.

Did she feel something for him? It was hard to believe, and yet... here she was, closed in a parlor with him and not Lord Stephen, the man she was supposed to be courting, who had been selected for her by her parents.

Which reminded him that their time was limited, and soon enough the rest of the party would come looking for her, and would likely notice that he was also absent. She might be interested in him enough for a kiss but certainly not enough for a lifetime.

When he broke the kiss, she leaned back, although her fingers were still gripping him as she breathed heavily, her eyes stroking up and down his body incredulously.

"Noah, I—I..."

"I'm sorry," he said roughly. "Perhaps I should not have done that."

"You *should* have," she countered. "I wanted it as much as you. I believe I made that obvious."

"You sound rather disbelieving."

She stepped back now, her fingers on her lips. "To be honest, I never saw it coming. We have known one another for some time, and yet, as of late... I have seen you in a different light."

He looked down at himself, some of his initial elation falling.

"Because I am someone else."

Her eyes flew up to his. "What do you mean?"

"My hair, my face, my clothing, my mannerisms – it is how you would like them. It is not me that you like, it is the man you have made me into, Lady Percy," he said, his disgust with himself lining his every word. Here he had made the mistake of thinking that such a woman was interested in him when, in truth, it was not him that she enjoyed. It was the idea of what she had created.

"That's not it at all," she said, shaking her head as she stepped forward.

"No?" he asked, raising a brow. "How is it, then, that it is only now you have noticed that I am more than just an acquaintance?"

She stopped with some hesitation. "It is only that as we have come to know one another better, I have a new awareness of you. It does not mean that I do not appreciate the man you are."

His lips quirked upward in a half-smile. "I do not believe you are being honest with me, Percy – or yourself," he said before he heard footsteps outside the door, and he turned his head toward the sound. "We should be getting back."

"But—"

"I will tell you when I have managed to get the necklace in my possession."

"Let me help you."

"There is no way you can help," he said, shaking his head. "It is not something that a young lady should be involved in."

"As opposed to all else that has occurred thus far?" she asked, her hands on her hips now as she challenged him.

"This could be dangerous. I will have to go at night, when I know Mrs. McNall will not be at home."

"Where does she live?"

"Walcot."

"Then it cannot be all bad. Tell me when."

"No."

"You are sore now, as your feelings have been hurt," she said, and his eyebrows rose at her forwardness, but then, this was part of what he liked about her. She lifted her arms to the side and then let them fall in obvious exasperation. "To be honest with you, Noah, I do not know why it is that you call to me, but you do. Can you not accept that?"

"Not really," he said simply. "I like to know why things are the way they are."

"Well, right now, we do not have time to discover that," she said, turning from him toward the door. "When I figure it out, you'll be the first to know. Tell me when you are going after the necklace. I'll be there."

With that, she pushed through the door, back toward the

drawing room, leaving him scratching his head once more, wondering what had just happened.

He waited a few moments before following her in, finding that Lord Stephen's eyes were on him as he walked toward the one seat that was open – between Miss Elizabeth and Percy herself on the small settee.

He finally met the man's gaze, not happy when he saw the gleam within it.

"Tell me, Mr. Rowley," Lord Stephen drawled out. "Where was it that I last saw you? I cannot quite recall."

"I believe it was at a social event," Noah said, wondering just where the man was going with this, for it would be all the worse for both of them if he named himself a patron of the notorious nightclub as well.

"Ah, yes, that's right. Except I do not believe I was there. I was just passing by."

"That can't be right," Lady Lecher said, leaning forward. "For we both saw you at the Assembly Rooms last week. For the fancy dress ball."

"I was there, yes," Noah said, inclining his head. "Perhaps you have me confused with another, Lord Stephen. I am told that I have one of those faces that is often mistaken."

"No, no, it was not the Assembly Rooms," Lord Stephen said, tapping a finger against his smirk. "I believe you were going into an establishment. One on a… quiet street."

Percy's eyes turned towards him, as she realized just exactly what Lord Stephen was saying. The only thing was, Lord Stephen had no idea that she was well aware of just what he was doing there.

"Yes, I saw you through a window," he continued. "You were quite close with a woman. Is she your betrothed?"

Feeling his aunt's stare, Noah managed a brittle smile. "As I said, you must have seen another and thought it was me. I am studying every day and the only evening social events I have attended have been with my aunt and uncle."

"And at night?"

"I remain in their home," Noah said, giving him a hard look, until finally Uncle Albert mercifully entered the conversation, asking Lord Fairfax about an investment, even though the women were obviously not pleased with the turn of conversation to business matters.

Noah felt Percy's eyes on him, and he looked up to meet her stare, surprised when she seemed upset. He had done nothing, and he had told her that.

So why didn't she believe him?

And why did it matter whether she did?

CHAPTER 14

None of this was going to plan.

Not their retrieval of the necklace, not her reaction to Lord Stephen, and certainly not what she was feeling about Noah.

Percy had to turn things around. And she was going to start tonight.

But first, she had to discover just what Noah was planning. She had a feeling that he was going to want to finish this as quickly as possible. The longer he waited, the more he would stew on everything. She was sure he would attempt to steal the necklace tonight.

She also knew that no matter what she asked him, he wasn't going to tell her his plans.

It was the night after the ill-fated dinner party that she had been so excited about, and she and her parents had retired earlier than usual, for no social events were occurring that evening.

Mary had already readied her for bed, but Percy removed her nightclothes as quickly as she could before donning a dark navy morning gown she found in the back of her wardrobe, one that was not fit for company but would do for tonight when she hoped to be invisible. She tied a black scarf around her hair before slowly and carefully opening her bedroom door, ensuring no one was about before she tiptoed through the corridor and down the stairs, watching for servants as she went.

She wished she was adventurous enough to sneak out her window, but she knew that would not likely end well.

Fortunately, the house Percy's family was renting was not far from Noah's aunt and uncle's home. She had discovered their address when they sent the invitation for dinner, and she had made sure that she knew where to find them. Keeping her head down, she was able to walk past the few people she encountered without notice.

Turning into the square, she slipped into the gardens, sitting on a bench in the dark. She looked over her shoulder every time she heard the smallest noise, trying to decide just what she would do if someone happened to discover her – be it a friendly surprise or a threat.

Fortunately, she didn't have long to wait before she saw Noah emerge from the front door, smiling when he looked from one side to the other surreptitiously– for it was not as though anyone else would have any awareness of what he was doing but this was quite out of character for him.

He was dressed, as she was, in dark colours, and he kept his hat low over his eyes as he walked down the street. Percy left her hiding place to follow him, her skirts swishing as she hustled to keep up with his quick pace.

He turned a few times, and Percy wished she was more familiar with Bath so that she had an idea as to where they were heading. Finally, he stopped in front of a well-kept house of an average size, as he once more checked for anyone watching him before he continued around the back.

Percy raced across the road, catching up to him just as he

stood on his toes to peer into the back window. She didn't want to startle him but needed him to realize she was there as she raised her hand and tapped her fingers on his shoulder.

"Noah," she hissed, and he whirled around in surprise, his hand on his chest.

"Percy!" he finally said with a gasp. "What are you doing?"

She placed her fists on her hips. "Did I not tell you to inform me as to when you were planning on stealing the necklace?"

"And I told you that I would do this myself," he hissed back.

"It will be much easier together."

"But—"

"I'm here now, so what difference does it make?" she asked, and he sighed, lifting his hat and running a hand through his hair.

"The difference is that if we are caught, there will be consequences. Ones that I do not even want to think of. I could extricate myself from the situation fairly easily, but what excuse would you have for being here?"

Percy bit her lip, worry finally creeping in.

"You have to make sure you are not found here," he said fiercely. "I'll take the blame if we are to be discovered."

"I do not need you to protect me," she said firmly. "I came here of my own accord. Now, boost me up and I'll see if I can fit through the window. I am rather curious as to how you thought to lift yourself high enough to open it alone."

She could tell she had him there, as he let out a grunt before he cupped his hands together for her foot, allowing her to step up and reach the window. She wished she was wearing breeches as she reached the top, letting out a groan of her own as she pushed the window up, relieved to find it unlocked.

"It seems our Mrs. MacNall is not as cautious as she should be," Percy murmured before sliding through, finding herself in a bedroom.

"Interesting," Noah said, surprising her from behind. He was light on his feet.

"What is?"

"This is not the bedroom I saw before."

"Is it not?"

"Do you suppose she lives with someone?" he asked, clearly as surprised as she, only Percy had an idea of the reason.

"Perhaps one is her own and the other is for... entertainment. I could understand the desire for a space that is hers and hers alone."

"Oh," he said, clearly shocked enough to stop his forward momentum, and she had to put a finger in his back to push him forward.

"On we go," she said. "Do you know which room it is in?"

"Yes."

"Lead the way."

It wasn't far, of course, the house not being overly large, and after they ensured that no one was home, Noah led them toward the room where had had seen the necklace, finding it darker than the rest of the house with only the smallest of embers burning in the grate.

Percy watched him enter.

"Do you think you can find it alone?"

"Yes. I came here alone, did I not?"

She ignored his barb, even though it was laced with humor, before she stepped forward. "I will keep watch. Keep your ears as vigilant as your eyes. We cannot be caught."

In the quiet darkness, she moved through the house to the front window, sinking low to keep watch in front. She could only hope that Mrs. MacNall wouldn't have reason to try any other entrance, that this was the most likely scenario.

Her heart was beating fast as she sat, which she knew was not only from the suspense of waiting but also from the very idea of what would happen if she was caught in this situation. Not only was she out, unchaperoned, in the middle of the night, but she had trespassed in a courtesan's house, accompanied by a young man. Even if he was the most scholarly and chivalrous man she had ever met, they would both face grave consequences for their actions.

Unless they managed to escape without being discovered.

"Noah?" she hissed. "Are you done?"

"I've found the key," he replied, his voice soft. "Now I just have to see where it fits."

She heard him mumbling to himself, heard the scratching of what must have been drawers within the wardrobe, until a further big sigh emerged.

"Are you having trouble?" she asked, even though the answer was obvious.

There was a pause. "Yes."

"Do you need help?"

Another pause. "Very well."

She quickly crossed the room, relieved that she could do something useful besides simply keeping watch.

He stepped back to allow her room to search within the wardrobe, and she ran her hand over the drawers. "There doesn't seem to be anything here that would work," she murmured. "Maybe…"

She searched farther down, along the bottom of the wardrobe, pleased when she found what she was looking for – a drawer within a drawer.

"Here," she said, and he nodded at her before drawing the key out from where he held it, fitting it into the lock. Percy didn't realize they were both holding their breath until they audibly sighed together once it worked.

She reached in, pulled out a mahogany box, and then opened the lid to reveal the ruby necklace within, shining up at them in all its glory.

"It really is beautiful, isn't it?" she said, and he nodded.

"Beautiful," he said, his voice thick, only, when she looked up and met his eyes, she found that he was not looking at the necklace but rather at her.

She swallowed, unable to look away—until they heard the click of a lock being turned. Their eyes widened in horror, as they heard the door open and footsteps begin to cross the floor.

"Under the bed," he said in a low, urgent voice, and she hurriedly shut the drawer and the wardrobe, keeping the necklace and the key in hand as she dove under the bed, Noah close behind her.

They lay there next to one another, staring up at the tight ropes beneath the mattress above them, until Percy had to close her eyes and take deep breaths, just as the sound of voices reached their ears.

"Percy?" Noah whispered. "Are you all right?"

"No," she whispered back. "I do not like small spaces. I feel as though the bed is going to collapse on top of me."

There was a warm tug on her hand, and she opened her eyes to find that Noah was holding her gaze as her hand remained secure within his own.

"Look at me," he commanded, and she turned her head toward him, finding his face just inches away. "It's just you and me," he said. "I won't let anything hurt you. Don't look up."

"But—"

"Percy," he said again, and she couldn't help but listen this time. The room was dim, but they were so close to one another, that she could see the circle of green that blended into the dark hazel of his eyes. She had never noticed that before, as she had never looked past his spectacles, she supposed. He had a few small freckles over his nose, and his lips were much fuller than she had imagined – although she already knew that, for she had felt them on her own. "I'm here. I will not let anyone hurt you."

She blinked, uncertain of where this side of him had come from.

His warm fingers curled tighter over hers and she held on, desperate for connection – but not just any connection. She wanted this closeness with him, Noah Rowley.

"Thank you," she whispered, but then suddenly the voices and footsteps drew closer, and her eyes widened and mouth opened in shock as she realized that Mrs. MacNall – and likely her lover – were in the room. Percy drew closer to Noah as though he could hide her from view, although she supposed it was smart to try to keep to the middle of the bed to minimize their chance of being seen.

"Where are you going?" came a deep voice, and Noah reached out, wrapping an arm around her.

"Lord Chesterham," he whispered in her ear.

Percy had to hide her slight squeak of surprise. For she had a very good idea for what purpose Lord Chesterham was here, and she wasn't entirely sure what she and Noah were supposed to do while it happened.

She could only hope that they were currently in the bedroom Mrs. MacNall considered her own – and that the other was for her liaisons.

"I am going to change into something more comfortable, darling," came Mrs. MacNall's sultry voice. "Pour yourself a drink and I will be out in a moment."

Her feet, clad in immaculate silky pink kid slippers with embroidered blue flowers that Percy would have liked for herself, appeared beside the bed behind Noah's head. Percy nodded her head toward them to signal him as to what was happening, and he just kept holding onto her gaze.

Fabric rustled before Mrs. MacNall cursed under her breath.

"Rosa? Can you come in, please?" she called, and Percy nearly choked. There had been servants here the entire time. How easily they could have been caught! How did a woman afford servants? It seemed that mistresses were much better paid than Percy had ever imagined.

The work boots of a maid appeared now, and she helped Mrs. MacNall remove the trappings of her dress and then don attire that was more appropriate for the occasion.

Mrs. MacNall said nothing to her maid, humming a song instead, her voice rich and melodic. It soothed Percy somewhat, who would have been in a panic if it were not for Noah's reassuring gaze upon her.

Finally, the woman walked out of the room, speaking to her lover again, in what Percy could only describe as purring. A strange jealousy began within her at the thought that Noah had been here with the woman, alone — until she remembered that he had left. For her.

The maid must have finished her tidying for she walked out of the room, hopefully to retire for the evening.

Lord Chesterham and Mrs. MacNall talked slightly longer until their voices trailed off, their footsteps coming closer, stopping outside the door, and suddenly the murmuring turned into heavy breathing and the whisper of fabric.

Oh, dear. Percy supposed she should have expected this. There was only one reason a man like Lord Chesterham would keep a mistress.

And it seemed they were going to be spectators for a show they hadn't counted on.

CHAPTER 15

This was agony.

Here he was, as close to Percy as he ever could have wanted to be, as close as he had only been in his dreams – and he was listening to another man seeking his satisfaction.

They had to get out of here. And they had to get out *now*.

But first, they had to determine which bedroom Mrs. MacNall and Lord Chesterham would put to use.

At the moment, they were using the wall in the corridor, if the panting and groaning were telling.

"On the bed," came the guttural command, and there were a few footsteps – away from where Noah and Percy were hiding. Thank goodness.

"Come, let's go," Noah whispered to Percy, scooting backward from under the bed, reaching a hand out to pull her with him. She took it, and when he finally had her out from under, he tried not to laugh at the dust covering her dark clothes.

He reached into his pocket and pulled out a small pouch filled with coins, which he left on top of the bed before turning back to Percy. It wasn't Mrs. MacNall's fault that she was losing such a valuable gift.

Keeping Percy's hand in his, he tugged her toward the window, lifting it up and then sliding out over the edge, grunting at the drop before he lifted his hands up toward her.

She swung one leg over the windowsill, and then froze when they heard a voice within— "Is something there?" Noah's heart seemed to stop, but Percy didn't hesitate as she jumped out, a sharp rip causing her momentum to slow. Her eyes widened but she landed in his arms before they looked up to see a large swath of her dress hanging out the window.

"Oh, dear," she said, but then looked at him with a shrug. "Nothing to be done now, but we'd better go."

Her scarf was askew, and he reached out, his fingers brushing the soft skin of her cheek as he straightened it over her hair, which would have been a sure giveaway if the light were to hit it just right.

Not that anyone would likely be watching for them right now, and Mrs. MacNall and Lord Chesterham were certainly otherwise occupied.

"Do you have the necklace?" he asked, and she nodded, lifting her hand to show him the box clutched within it.

"I've had it the whole time."

"Good," he said tersely. "Let's go."

They started down the street at a fast pace, although he made sure to slow enough to accommodate her skirts. Fortunately, she had worn good boots, and he had to commend her forethought, even if accompanying him had been foolhardy.

"Where are we going?" she asked, and he turned to her in surprise.

"I'm taking you home."

"Not yet!" she protested. "We have to inspect the necklace."

"Percy, do you know what time it is?"

"I'd say shortly after midnight."

"Far past time for me to return you."

"At this point, everyone is sleeping. Another hour or two won't change anything," she said, her smile obviously meant to convince him, and it annoyed him that it was working. "Where can we go?"

"Percy, if you are caught—"

"We've escaped capture so far, though, have we not?" she asked with that gleam in her eye that made him forget all of his protestations and go along with whatever she suggested. He sighed. He knew that agreeing to this was ill-advised, except not only did it mean more time with her, but he did want to inspect the necklace himself and he had a feeling she wouldn't let him do so without her.

"Very well," he said. "My aunt and uncle are attending an engagement and they usually stay out until the early hours of the morning. We could return to their home."

"Wonderful!" she said, turning onto their square and he stopped.

"How do you know where they live?"

"I followed you from here," she said simply, and he couldn't help but laugh as he shook his head.

"How did you know I would go tonight?"

"Just a guess," she said, bumping her shoulder into his. "I feel that I am coming to know you well enough to guess your movements."

He had no retort for that but rather had to swallow the lump in his throat. He was also enjoying the intimacy they shared, but he was worried that it would only lead him to a bitter heart when this was all over and she went on her way.

"Wait here," he said when they reached the house, and

he ascended first, opening the door to ensure no servants were about. From what he knew, most of them retired for the night until his aunt and uncle returned. He waved Percy in, and she slipped up the steps and through the door, staying silent as he led her down the corridor and up the staircase.

"We are best to go into my bedchamber if you don't mind. I know it is far from appropriate, but it is the place where we are least likely to be discovered."

She stopped on the top step, smiling up at him. "I trust you, Noah."

He nodded, though he wondered if she would say the same if she knew the imaginings racing around his mind at the thought of what he would truly like to do with her in a bedroom.

They had been in the room for less than a minute when there was a knock on the door.

Percy turned to him with wide eyes, looking back and forth, and he gestured to the wardrobe.

Once she was standing behind it and out of sight, Noah answered it, relieved to find only his valet on the other side.

"I do not need anything this evening," he said. "Retire for the night, Andrews."

His valet rubbed the sleep from his eyes as he wished him a good night, and Noah breathed a sigh of relief as he shut the door and locked it for good measure.

When he turned around, he found that Percy was standing over the foot of the bed, upon which she had placed the box that held the necklace.

He walked over to stand beside her, and together, their fingers brushing, they opened the box to look down upon the necklace once more.

"It's beautiful," Percy breathed. "I can see why Cassandra's aunt had it hidden for so long."

"I wish I knew how it was stolen," Noah said. "I feel as though that would answer many of our questions."

"Likely, yes," Percy said. "But unless you can convince Mrs. MacNall to tell you who gave it to her, we will be out of luck."

"Do you think she will guess that I was the one to take it?" Noah asked as the question had been gnawing at him for some time. "How much of a coincidence is it that you and I both asked about the necklace and the next night it goes missing?"

"We could blame it on one of her servants."

"Then I'm sure she would remove them from her employment, which would hardly be fair."

"You're right," Percy said, catching her lip between her teeth, and Noah longed to reach out and soothe the pink skin where she bit it. "You are a good man, Noah."

"A practical one," he corrected her, even as his heart warmed at her words.

When she tilted her head up toward him, her face was again just inches away. By this point, he had memorized every detail of it – every freckle, every plane of her face, every ring of color in her blue-green eyes.

The air seemed to still between them, the only sound their intermingling breath.

He leaned in a fraction, and she did the same – but then a crack in the fireplace had them both jumping, breaking apart.

"The jewels," he said in the thick, heated air, and she nodded.

"The jewels," she repeated in a breathy voice as she lifted the necklace out of its box once more.

She passed it to him, and he held it close, taking off his spectacles so he could better see it in front of his face. As he had imagined, there, in front of him, was what he'd spotted upon his all-too-brief examination earlier – a small hole in the gold backing of the ruby heart.

He reached into his pocket, pulling out the key that he had kept with him since arriving in Bath. He held it up before pushing it into the small hole – and he was surprised when it pressed down, then turned.

He looked up, and while Percy's face was blurred in front of him, he could sense her staring at him. He turned the key.

As he did, a piece of the necklace swung down, revealing a hollow space.

"Is there something inside?" Percy asked, dipping her head to see, her body now just inches from his.

"I think so," he said, tilting the necklace, causing a piece of paper to slide out as he did. He tried to reach it, but his fingers were too big. He passed it to Percy and watched her long, slim fingers reach within and pull out a small, brittle piece of paper.

"What does it say?" he asked, and held out his hand.

"Not much of anything," she said. "Just a name."

"San Sebastian," he read before returning his spectacles to his face. "What could that mean?"

She shrugged. "I couldn't say. Perhaps Cassandra or Lord Ashton might know more?"

"One can only hope," he muttered, before replacing the paper. "We have it now, at least. We have done our part. I should return the necklace to Mrs. Compton."

"I can do so tomorrow, if you'd like."

"Shall we go together?" he asked, desperate for another opportunity to see her.

"I'd be happy to," she said with a small smile before looking around his bedchamber. It was of an average size, and he had been comfortable here since he had arrived, although he certainly hadn't made it home yet. Perhaps that was because he would not be staying long. The more time he spent discovering various sources in these Bath homes, the more he was looking forward to returning to London and adding them to the wealth of knowledge he was building.

"Well," Percy said, clearing her throat, and breaking the sudden tension that had filled the air. "I suppose I best be going now."

"I will walk you home."

"You don't have to."

"Of course I do," he said indignantly. "I could never allow you to walk alone."

"Because you feel responsible for me?" she asked, looking up at him now with something in her eyes that he felt resembled need – but it couldn't be. Not for him. He wasn't the strong, aggressive man that she longed for. He was a man who enjoyed history, the already known, order, a quiet life. He couldn't provide her the excitement she craved, nor the strength she preferred. It was good to continue to remind himself of that.

But, if necessary, he could be her friend – even if he would spend the rest of his life longing for more.

"Thank you, Noah," she said simply, interrupting his thoughts.

"For what?"

"For watching out for me. For allowing me to come with you. For not treating me like a child or as someone who does not know her own mind."

"You have a much more interesting mind than any other I have come across."

"That is quite kind of you, although it is nothing compared to your own."

She surprised him by stepping forward, causing him to catch his breath.

"Shall we go?" he asked.

"Yes," she breathed, but instead of moving toward the

door, she inched closer to him, until he had no option but to bring his hands up and around her waist.

"Percy?" he said as she tilted her head back and stared up at him, her blue eyes wide.

"Yes?"

"I—" But before he could say anything, could tell her that this was a terrible idea, her lips met his, pressing against them in question.

And the only answer he could give her was yes.

A thousand times yes.

CHAPTER 16

Percy was known for being forward, but this—this was more than she had even expected of herself.

But she could no longer disregard the tension that had been growing between them all night – all week, if she was being honest. So she did what she always did and faced the situation head on. She needed this man, and she needed him now.

And no one was more surprised about it than she was.

She knew that this was everything she had been warned against – the reason why her mother would have forbidden the books she read with her friends. She wasn't married to Noah, nor even betrothed or courting.

Percy enjoyed her time with Noah, of course she did, but she could hardly imagine marrying him. He was a scholar who was going to write history, for goodness' sake. Her family had other plans for her, and as much as she tried to deny them, she knew that at some point she would have to agree to a man they chose for her.

That didn't mean, however, that she couldn't enjoy this with Noah – even as a niggling thought reminded her that he was not the man who would do this with a woman like her without considering what might come next.

That didn't change the fact that she wanted nothing more than to be in his arms, in his bed, his body in hers.

She had a feeling he might not approve, nor take what she was ready to give – but she was willing to find out.

Knowing him for some time, Percy would have expected that Noah's kiss would have been soft, hesitant, patient.

But it was none of that. Not at all.

Once her lips touched his, he paused for a moment, as though uncertain of whether or not he would return her touch. Once his decision was made, however, he answered her with complete abandon of the personality he had always presented to the world, overjoying her.

As abruptly as he kissed her, he pulled back, although he didn't completely break off with her as he had in the past.

"I should take you home."

Her eyes wandered over his face, her breath coming in short pants.

"You should."

He didn't move toward the door. Neither did she.

He reached up, his hands cupping her head, but instead of pulling her in toward him, he trailed his fingers over her face, the pads of his thumbs softly gliding down her cheeks. His gentle touch was causing as much turmoil within her as his passionate kisses had, and she closed her eyes for a moment to try to ease all of the resulting sensations.

He tilted his head then, lowering his lips toward hers once more, and she eagerly met him halfway, placing her hands on his chest, feeling the steady beat of his heart against her fingers. That's what he was – steady. She could trust him, could count on him, could know that he would always be true to his word and support her in not only what he thought was right, but what she did as well. In all of their acquaintance, he had never let her down.

And she knew that he wouldn't now.

She kissed him back with as much fervor as he. She turned off her mind, forgetting everything but the two of them, together in this room. There was no treasure to find, no necklace to steal, no friends to answer to, no matches to make.

It was Percy and Noah, and the heat that was threatening to consume them both.

His knee nudged her legs apart ever so slightly, and she had the urge to lean in and rock against him, as his hands kneading into her back only left her aching for him from where he touched her to where his knee rested.

She wasn't thinking when she undid the buttons of his waistcoat. When she lifted his shirt out of his breeches. When she coasted her hands beneath it and slid them up.

When her fingers found the light dusting of hair that led a trail from his chest to disappear beneath his breeches, the room spun slightly. Percy had always imagined that Noah was rather slight, which made many consider him weak. But he was not weak at all. His body was made up of sinewy muscle, his every abdominal plane a ridge beneath her fingers, his chest hard yet welcoming at the same time.

"Percy," he groaned against her lips, her name coming out as both a prayer and a curse.

"Is something the matter?" she asked, a bolt of confidence bursting through her as she leaned in and took his earlobe between her teeth.

He hissed and she giggled, enjoying the power she had over him.

She rocked slightly against him, testing him to see what he'd do, and he surprised her by reaching his hands around her and holding her hips close toward him so that she couldn't move, although his fingers dug into her bottom.

"I can't stop thinking about you," he said, his breath coming hard, and she closed her eyes.

"I have similar thoughts," she admitted. "I don't know why."

When she opened her eyes once more, he was smiling grimly. "Does that trouble you?"

"No," she said honestly. "I just don't understand it. Why do you do this to me when no other man ever has?"

"Perhaps it is my spectacles," he said, arching a brow. "Or my scent of dusty old libraries."

"You don't smell of books," she said before she could stop herself. "You smell of spice and ink."

"Is that a good thing?" he asked, laughter in his voice and she nodded.

"I would say it is."

He kissed her again, and she was shocked at the response of her body, which immediately stiffened beneath his fingers.

He made her *feel* – physically, of course, but it was more than that. He made her feel alive, womanly, desirable.

Noah kissed down the side of her face, her neck, her collarbone, until his face was nestled in the top of her bodice.

"Yes," she breathed, "kiss me there."

He acquiesced, and just when she wondered how his mouth would feel on her nipple, he freed one of her breasts from her dress and sucked it. She gasped as the sensation was connected all the way to the most tender place between her legs.

"Noah," she breathed as he filled all of her senses. "More."

She needed him and all that he could give her. She knew there was more, both from the books she had read and the yearning she felt for fulfillment when she brushed against him, when he kissed her neck and her mouth and her throat.

She wished there was no clothing between them, wished she could feel his body against hers.

"Percy, stop."

"Stop?"

She didn't like that word, especially at this moment, and pulled back to tell him exactly that, but she soon realized that he didn't mean to stop entirely – he was simply removing his jacket and waistcoat, folding them and placing them on the bed before turning back to her, his eyes dark, hooded – hungry.

"Lie down," he said gruffly, and her eyes widened. Noah Rowley was going to make love to her.

She had imagined this moment in so many ways – but never like this, never with a man like him.

And yet, she wasn't sure that anything could ever be more perfect.

Percy did as he asked, lying down on the bed, although she held herself up on her elbows, too curious about what he was planning to do to completely give herself over. He followed her like a hunter after its prey, climbing over her – but not all the way up. Instead, he stopped, lifted her skirts – and then dived beneath them.

"What are you doing?" she asked, instantly shocked out of her languid passion.

"I am giving you the pleasure you deserve."

"I deserve?"

"That you deserve," he repeated, before pausing a beat. "And that I must give you."

"But—"

His head appeared over the layers of fabric.

"Do you trust me?"

"Yes," she answered without hesitation.

A rare grin crossed his face as he reached up and removed his spectacles, placing them on the table beside them. "Good," he said, and then disappeared from her sight once more.

His hands came to her thighs, spreading them apart, holding her open to him, and then at the first stroke of his tongue, her entire body nearly arched off the bed.

"Noah!" she cried out, but when he lifted a hand and placed a finger over her lips, she clamped them close together, although she couldn't help the soft moans that escaped her as he continued. At first, it was nearly too much as she squirmed beneath him, but she began to relax into it – although it wasn't long until an intensity was building within her, one that was so incredible she almost wondered how it could be possible.

It happened so fast, so forcefully that she nearly cried. As the sensations flooded through her, she had to grab a pillow and place it over her face, biting into the fabric to try to stem the emotion that was spilling through her lips.

Her eyes were still closed when Noah's weight dipped the bed beside her, and she wished she could keep her eyes closed, for she was suddenly far too shy to look at him.

But then he reached out and trailed his fingers over her cheek, turning her head towards him.

"Percy?" he said in a low voice. "Are you all right?"

She had no choice but to open her eyes then, and she knew that she'd had nothing to fear. His expression was reassuring and languid, and she wondered how she had missed this man for so long.

"I am more than all right," she said dreamily. "I am... floating."

He chuckled, lying down beside her, and she sat up, her energy slowly returning.

She unbuttoned the top of his shirt and trailed her fingers down his exposed chest, wanting to see what she had only felt before.

"Percy…" he reached up, grabbing her fingers. "What are you doing?"

"You got to play," she said coyly. "Now it's my turn."

She tried to tug her hand away, but he only held it firmer. "You don't have to," he said, shaking his head, and she sat up before straddling his hips, pushing him down, one hand on his chest.

"I know that," she retorted, "but I want to."

He leaned back then, crossing his arms behind his head, giving himself to her.

She smiled wickedly. In this moment, he was hers.

And she was going to take full advantage of it.

CHAPTER 17

Noah had lived this moment in his fantasies, but he had never been naïve enough to think it could come true.

The woman of his dreams was on top of him, having her way with him. He knew that he should tell her to stop, that she was an unmarried young lady who should maintain her innocence – but he couldn't find it within him to do so.

Besides that, she seemed to be enjoying herself.

He closed his eyes, losing himself to the sensation of her fingers on his chest. Soon her lips followed, pressing them to his mouth before moving to his ear, his neck, and then she was lifting his shirt off of his body. He helped her, taking his arms out, before collapsing on the bed once more as she kissed her way down, leaving gooseflesh in her wake.

When she reached the fall of his breeches, he lifted his hands, either to push her away or help her, he wasn't sure, but she swatted them away and went to work herself, unfastening them and then sliding them down his legs.

She paused, sitting up for a moment, and when he opened his eyes, she was staring at him, her gaze riveted on his cock before she reached out and ran her fingers slowly over his flesh. It took all of his control not to come at her mere touch.

"Percy," he pleaded in supplication, although for what, he wasn't entirely certain. Then she shifted, moving down his body, and lowered her head, wrapping her lips around him and bobbing up and down. He groaned, and she quickly sat up.

"Is this all right?" she asked, and he could only nod, no longer able to form any coherent words. He could tell she was uncertain, and he reached down, gently moving her head to show her what to do.

She was a quick student, and it wasn't long until she was moving of her own accord, swirling her tongue over him as she moved up and down.

He tried as hard as he could to hold back, but his response overwhelmed him, and it wasn't long before his climax began to build within him.

"Percy," he panted. "Percy, stop, I'm going to come."

Stop, she didn't, however. She only increased her efforts, until he couldn't hold back any longer and was spending into her mouth. Her fingers dug into his thighs, holding on until he finished, and when she sat up, her cheeks were pink and her eyes glossy.

"I'm sorry," he said, earning himself a swat across the chest.

"For what? For allowing me to do what I wanted?"

"Yes?" He wasn't certain of the correct response, but at the moment it seemed best to agree with her.

"Noah, I do not think I have ever felt so alive before," she said, looking like a goddess as she sat up, her hair now mostly down around her shoulders, shimmering in the lamplight. "Can I tell you something?"

"Anything."

"I cannot wait until we can do it again."

***

NOAH COULD HARDLY CONTAIN the bounce in his step as he strode up to Percy's family's house the next day. He should be exhausted, considering he had only slept a few hours, but instead, he was invigorated by the most perfect woman he had ever met, who seemed to, against all rational thought, want him.

As much as he would have loved nothing more than to keep her in his bed for the rest of the night, to hold her close and tell her everything he admired about her, all that he wanted to do to her, rational thought had prevailed and he had walked her home after they had dressed, careful to keep her hood up and draped around her face to prevent anyone from identifying them on their walk home. She had snuck into her house through a window, and he hoped that she had made it to her chamber without any notice.

Today they were to return the necklace to Mrs. Compton, but he had nearly forgotten about their mission, so intent was he on Percy herself.

He raised his hand to knock on the door, but she opened it before he could rap even once.

"Noah!" she said brightly – too brightly. "There you are."

"All is well?" he asked, and she nodded, although her smile didn't quite reach her eyes.

"Yes, of course. My maid will accompany us this morning."

They began the short walk to Mrs. Compton's, a stilted silence suddenly stretching between them.

"About last night—" he began, but she held up a hand to stop him.

"It was wonderful," she said, her smile warm and true now. "Thank you."

That seemed to be all she wished to say on the subject, so

he returned to the matter before them, holding up the box in his hands.

"How will we explain this to Mrs. Compton?"

She tilted her head to the side.

"From what I have seen of the woman, I suggest we tell her the truth."

He wasn't sure about admitting to their theft, but followed Percy's lead as she knocked on the door, the butler allowing them entrance. As they waited for Mrs. Compton, Noah took the opportunity to wander the room, studying the many artifacts that lined the shelves.

He was interested, yes, but he also knew that if he spent too much time sitting next to Percy, he might be inclined to do something he shouldn't – like claim her as his own.

They had shared a night of passion, but that didn't mean she would be ready to leave her life and what was expected of her to be with a man like him. She had made it very clear that she was interested in a powerful man – in more ways than just physical – a description he did not match.

"Lady Persephone and Mr. Rowley."

Noah turned when Mrs. Compton strode into the room, her wrapper floating behind her, her black hair with its grey streaks piled high on her head like a crown.

"How lovely for you to visit me again." She paused. "Mr. Rowley, you are looking quite fine."

Percy beamed in obvious pride. Noah cringed slightly at the reminder that Percy had only become interested in him since she had recreated his image into a man of her liking. "He does, doesn't he?"

"I apologize that our last conversation ended in such a dreary manner."

Percy stood, clasping her hands together, clearly excited to share their news with Mrs. Compton. "As it happens, we have come to fix that."

"Whatever do you mean?" Mrs. Compton asked, sitting next to Percy on the sofa, while Noah remained standing by the window, his hands clasped behind his back.

"After we left, we decided that we wanted to right the injustice that had been done to you," Percy said, causing Noah to raise a brow. Obviously, Percy was not going to share the *entire* truth. "We were at an event one evening shortly after and saw a woman wearing a necklace we were certain was yours."

"Who is this woman?" Mrs. Compton asked, standing now.

"It doesn't matter," Percy said hurriedly, and Noah appreciated that she saw fit to protect Mrs. MacNall. "It was given to her. However, we knew it didn't rightfully belong to her so…"

Percy reached out, picking up the box off the table where they had left it. She held it out toward Mrs. Compton.

"We retrieved it for you."

Mrs. Compton reached out, her hands slightly shaking as she opened the box, gasping when she saw the necklace within, running her fingers over it.

"My rubies," she said, looking up at them, her lips parted in surprise. "But how—"

"It doesn't matter how," Percy said, shaking her head slightly. "I am only happy that we could return them to you."

"Thank you," Mrs. Compton said, looking down as she appeared to be overwhelmed with emotion. "Thank you ever so much. These are special to me for many reasons. They have been in my family for years, of course, and contain much history. They are also very valuable. But more than that, they—"

She stopped, shaking her head, suddenly realizing that she was, perhaps, saying too much.

"We have Cassandra's confidence," Percy said gently,

THE SCHOLAR'S KEY

placing her hand on Mrs. Compton's arm as she sat back down.

"They were passed down to me with clear instructions," she said softly. "I was to always keep them in my possession, to never sell them or give them away. It was never made clear why, only that it was important to keep them safe."

Percy looked back at Noah, who shook his head. He could understand Percy's desire to share with Mrs. Compton her own family's story, but it wasn't their place to do so. It should come from her niece and nephew.

"I am happy that we were able to return them," Percy said. "They're beautiful."

"Although you should, perhaps, consider, just how they were stolen," Noah said pragmatically. "Can you trust everyone in your household?"

"I should hope so," Mrs. Compton said, although she appeared troubled. Percy shot Noah a look of displeasure, as though she didn't like that he was questioning the woman's domestic help, but, if anything, concluding who the culprit was could prevent them from being stolen again.

He caught Mrs. Compton's intuitive glance between them and realized she had sensed the silent conversation they were having. Her gaze turned speculative.

"Come," she said, dimples appearing in her cheeks. "I have something I should like to show you."

With a swish of her skirts and the shawl she wore around her shoulders, she sailed from the room, and Percy and Noah had no choice but to follow her down the hall and up the stairs. Noah moved to the side to allow Percy to go ahead of him, closing his eyes and revelling in her scent as she floated by him.

When Mrs. Compton turned into what appeared to be a bedchamber, Noah stopped.

"I am not sure that I—"

"Come," she said, waving him forward. "I have no secrets to hide."

He stepped into the room with hesitation, moving no farther forward than the threshold, while Percy followed the woman in, amusement on her face. Mrs. Compton opened a drawer in her wardrobe, pulling out a soft velvet bag.

"I want you to know how much I appreciate you returning my necklace to me," she said, laying the bag on the bed before lifting it to deposit its contents on the quilt. "I'd like you to have these."

She held out a pair of gold rings, passing the wider, thicker one to Noah and the matching, thinner one to Percy.

Percy held hers in her palm, staring at Mrs. Compton with surprise. "Thank you, Mrs. Compton. We are truly honored, but we cannot take these," she said shaking her head and trying to pass them back, but Mrs. Compton lifted her hands.

"Bring them downstairs," she said, waving to the door. "I shall tell you a story, but the young man is not comfortable in an old lady's bedchamber."

She laughed as she passed him, Percy grinning along with her, and soon enough they had returned to the drawing room. Noah kept the ring fisted tightly in his hand, uncertain of just what he was supposed to do with it. He supposed it was best to simply follow Percy's lead, as she seemed to have a much better grasp of conventions in such situations.

"Now," Mrs. Compton said, settling her vibrant skirts around her legs while a maid set a tea tray on the table. "Let me tell you about these rings. My husband, as you likely know, was a merchant. He was well-to-do, but not of noble blood. My father had chosen another man for me to wed. He was a fine enough sort, but he didn't cause me any great feeling. Not like my Robert did." She smiled wistfully. "I used to sneak out of the house at night to meet Robert in the garden behind our London townhouse. He was in Parliament, you see, so he spent a great deal of time in London. My father never knew."

Percy was leaning forward, holding onto every word of the romantic tale. "Where did you first meet?" she asked.

"We met at Vauxhall," Mrs. Compton said with a smile. "I had become lost in the gardens, and he was my saviour. Anyway," she continued, waving a hand, "we ran away to be married when my father didn't immediately agree to the wedding. Can you believe we went all the way to Gretna Green?" She chuckled. "Robert bought the rings before he even knew I would marry him. He had them engraved with the sign of infinity and said that they would always remind us of how our souls would be intertwined, no matter what happened to us or who I married." She looked up at them. "I'd like you to have them, truly I would."

Percy's eyes were bright as she blinked back the tears that appeared to be nearly spilling over. "We could never," she said. "They mean so much to you."

"They do," Mrs. Compton replied. "And that is why I think they should go to someone else, as a reminder of what you have together."

"Oh, but we—" Percy cut a look over to Noah.

His jaw tightened. He knew what she was going to say. That they were not together, not a couple, and never would be. He understood, and he agreed with her. They shouldn't take these rings. But then he noticed Mrs. Compton's expression, so full of hope.

Percy must have realized the same, for she dropped her head. "Thank you," she said simply.

When they had left the house, promising to call again before they departed Bath, Noah looked over at her.

"What will you do with the ring?" he asked.

"Wear it, I suppose," she said, holding it up. "I cannot seem to fit it on my finger, however."

"Here," he said when he watched her struggle once more to slide it on. "Let me."

He took the ring from her, holding her hand in his while he fit the ring onto her fourth finger, turning it just enough that it slid down to where it was supposed to be.

"There," he said, reluctantly dropping her hand, and she tugged her glove back on overtop of it. "Perfect fit."

He fit the ring on his own finger.

"You are keeping yours, then?" she asked, looking up at him from beneath her long eyelashes.

"I figured my finger was the best place to keep from losing it," he said gruffly. He didn't want to say it, but he knew without a doubt that he would never part with the ring, not when it was such a tie to the one Percy wore. "Tell me what you choose to do with yours, however, for they should be together."

"I agree," she said softly as they began the return walk to the townhouse. Noah wished he could lean in closer to her, at least take her hand – even if it meant nothing to her – but her maid was trailing behind them, and he didn't want to risk anything that might get Percy into any sort of trouble or would force her to agree to a promise that she wouldn't want to keep.

He walked her up the front steps of the house, but she turned to him before they came to the landing.

"Thank you, Noah," she said, her eyes darting back and forth behind him, and he frowned. Was she trying to get rid of him so quickly? Did she not want to be seen with him? "I appreciate... everything."

"Persephone!" came a call from within as the door opened, revealing her mother. "There you are. Where have you been? Our guests arrived over an hour ago!"

Her mother hadn't even seen him. Percy gave him one more smile – a regretful one, perhaps? – before the door closed behind her.

Leaving Noah to wonder if that was the last he would ever see of her.

CHAPTER 18

*P*ercy knew she shouldn't have left the house. Not after her parents' request. But she hadn't been able to resist the chance to see Noah and finish this quest they had begun together. She had hoped that she would feel relieved now that they had found their clue and returned the necklace, but instead, she was only more unsettled than ever before.

And the biggest reason for that was standing in front of her.

"Lord Stephen, it is lovely to see you," she said, even though she wasn't being entirely honest. When her mother had told her that Lord Stephen was calling, she had honestly hoped to miss the visit.

"And you, Lady Persephone."

"Lady Percy is just fine," she said, not enjoying how her full name sounded from his mouth. Somehow, it hadn't sounded quite so vile when it had rolled off of Noah's lips.

"Very well," he said, his eyes lighting up, and she realized she had given him the wrong impression, for now, he thought she was inviting him to become much more familiar with her.

She looked around the drawing room, disconcerted when she realized that her father was there as well. Why were both her parents here, as well as Lord Stephen's? Her stomach began to roil, and she tried to think of a way out of this. She knew she would have to be more forward in dismissing his suit — at least until she was sure — but to do it in front of both families would only bring disgrace upon both of them.

"Should we go for a walk?" she asked, clasping her hands together. "It is quite a lovely day. I was just outside myself and—"

"We have something we should like to discuss first," her father interjected. "Perhaps you should sit down, Percy."

Unfortunately, the only seat was the one beside Lord Stephen on the settee, and she sat but tried to keep her distance, even as he only seemed to draw closer toward her. Her skin crawled at the formality coating the room, and she wished with all her might she was anywhere but here – although if she had to choose, she would be with Noah. He was often silent, and contemplative, but there was no unease there. Only safety. He was… home.

"Lord Stephen and I had an excellent conversation earlier," her father said, crossing one leg over the other, getting straight to the point. "He asked me if he could have your hand. I agreed."

Time seemed to stand still as they all sat there, staring at her as disconcertingly as the wax figurines she had seen at Madame Tussaud's. Finally, she realized that they were waiting for her to say something.

"My… hand?" she managed. The hand that was currently covered in a glove but wore a ring matching the one upon Noah's. It seemed to connect them, even though it was only a material item.

"In marriage," her father finished as though she might have misunderstood.

"I see," she said, wishing with all her might that her father had discussed this with her without Lord Stephen and his parents present. She swung a glance over to her mother, who had promised that she would get a say in who she married, but her mother gave a nearly imperceptible shrug along with her pitying gaze. It seemed that she had not been able to stretch her father's patience any longer.

"That is... most flattering," she said, her voice nearly squeaking.

"It is, isn't it?" her father said with a look that was obviously meant to convince her to accept. "I have told him and his father that we would be most interested in such a complimentary match. You have known one another for so long."

Percy shifted back and forth on the sofa, as Lord Stephen leaned in. He really was handsome. He had a chiselled jaw, dark hair that swept over his brow in the most becoming fashion, dark eyes, and a figure that would have rivalled that of Hercules.

She thought back to what she and Noah had done together, how they had explored one another's bodies, how he had made her feel as though the entire earth was shaking with his touch. She closed her eyes, trying to picture Lord Stephen's face, his hands doing that to her instead – and she shuddered.

She didn't realize that she had done so visibly until she looked around the room and saw her mother's concern, her father's anger, Lord and Lady Lecher's confusion, and Lord Stephen's annoyance.

She swallowed hard.

"You must understand that I am most appreciative of this offer, I truly am. It is such a life-changing decision, however, and I am wondering if I might have a few days to think on this?" Her father started to speak, and she laid a hand on his arm as she tried to placate him – and everyone else in the room. "Perhaps, in the meantime, Lord Stephen and I might spend some time together to get to know one another and see if we might suit?"

She smiled the smile that had always worked on her father. He was a hard man to most, but deep down, he had a weakness for her that he tried not to show to anyone else.

He frowned but looked over to Lord Lecher.

"Is that agreeable, Lecher?"

The viscount did not look particularly pleased, but as Percy's father outranked him and he was likely most interested in his family acquiring her sizeable dowry, he nodded woodenly. "Very well."

The family stood before taking their leave, and Percy wished she could also slip out the door and run away. She stood as still as she could, staring out the window, although her back prickled as she felt her parents waiting.

"Well?" her father said, and she turned around slowly, finding him standing there with his arms crossed. "What have you to say for yourself?"

"Father, I appreciate that you are trying to make a good match for me, truly I do," she said, her gaze flicking over to her mother for help, but her mother stood off to the side, her head slightly bowed. "I thought, however, that I would have some input in who I choose for a husband. Perhaps if you had discussed this with me alone, before—"

"Enough," her father growled, and she jumped, even though his tone wasn't loud, but rather even. Her father was not one particularly given to any emotion, but it seemed in this he was determined. "I did say you could have input, but that was two seasons ago. You are not only unmarried, but you have shown no interest in any man. What are you going to do, spend the rest of your life living with your brother?"

She tilted her head to the side. "Well, if he will allow it, then—"

Her father snorted. "Your brother needs to find a wife of his own, and he will have little chance of that if he has another woman living in his house. Especially a woman like you."

"A woman like me?" she repeated as an ache began to creep into her chest.

"A woman like you, yes," her father said. "One who speaks her mind, who doesn't know her place, who is impertinent and defies what is expected of her."

He was heated now, and Percy knew better than to continue to push him, but pain sliced through her at his words. She had thought that her father would always be there for her, that they had a bond that was stronger than the expectations placed upon them by society.

"Harold," her mother said softly, trying to stop him, but that only earned her his anger.

"It's your fault," he said, pointing at her mother now. "You have been too indulgent with her."

Her mother lifted her chin, stepping forward. "Have you asked Percy if she is interested in any *other* man?" she said, turning to Percy and nudging her chin forward in encouragement.

Percy bit her lip uneasily. Her mother couldn't be referring to Noah – could she? However, he had called upon her a few times, and when they had been at social events, Percy had spent more time with him than any other man. She was sure that wouldn't have gone unnoticed by her mother.

"I... have some interest, yes," she said slowly, and her father stared at her intently.

"Does he return this interest?"

Percy was about to say yes but then paused. She had assumed that Noah felt something for her by the way that he had acted with her, but she didn't know what that something was. Was it friendship? Lust? She couldn't be certain.

"I am not entirely sure," she said truthfully.

"Who is it?"

"I would not like to say until I know how he feels in turn," she said, and her father sighed, waving his hand toward her, apparently having given up.

"Do what you must. I need an answer in two days. In the meantime, spend some time with Lord Stephen. He is a good man, from a good family. I do think, Percy, that if you open yourself to the possibility, you might be pleasantly surprised."

"And he is ever so handsome," her mother added.

With one last shake of his head, her father left the room.

Her mother turned to her with an eyebrow raised, taking Lord Stephen's seat on the settee and patting the cushion beside her. "Come sit and tell me about Mr. Rowley."

"There isn't much to tell," Percy said with a shrug as she did as her mother bid. "We have spent time together, and I do enjoy his company. However, even if he was interested in pursuing a romance with me – which, I would have thought he would have expressed that interest by now – he is a second son, one who spends his days with his nose in books, searching through old letters and diaries. I can hardly imagine Father approving."

"Perhaps not," her mother said thoughtfully, "but you never know. Perhaps he would surprise you. I believe that part of your father's newfound insistence on your marriage stems from his concern that you will not be looked after."

"I will always find my way," Percy said, sitting as tall as she could.

"I know that," her mother said, patting her hand. "But we would both like to make certain that you are taken care of. No one should be alone, Percy."

With a squeeze of Percy's hand, she stood and walked out of the room, leaving Percy to consider her future.

She had always considered Noah a friend, and when they had practiced flirtation, she had become more aware of him than ever before. It was not, in hindsight, the flirting that had made him attractive to her, nor even his change in looks. It had caused her to *notice* him, and once she had, she'd liked what she had seen. He was not at all what she had thought she wanted in a man, but she had come to realize that she liked the fact he was introspective, that he put other people first, and that he carefully assessed every situation. He was warm, safe, and steady, and she knew that she would always be able to count on him – something that could not be said about most people.

But was it enough to build a life together? And what would he have to say about it?

One decision could change everything.

But before she took that step forward, there was one question she needed answered.

Whether Noah felt anything for her.

CHAPTER 19

Noah sat at the breakfast table, opening the paper before him. It had become his custom to read the news of the day with his first meal, and he would then go continue his research. He enjoyed this life, this routine. He could see a future like this. There was only one thing missing.

Percy.

For a moment – just a moment – he allowed himself to picture her waking up next to him, her hair tousled and her smile satiated, before she would sit at the table beside him to begin their day together. Perhaps there could be children, if he was ever so lucky. Then he would continue his work, doing something that fulfilled him, for as long as it might take.

He ran a hand over his face, washing the image away.

Because it wasn't meant to be. So there was no point in even considering it.

He was not the type of man she had an interest in. She was only giving him any attention at all because she had made him into a shadow of a man she desired. She didn't care for who he truly was, and that was all he wanted – a woman who loved him for himself.

However, that didn't change the fact that he couldn't stop thinking about her, that he went to sleep with her on his mind and woke up with her in his heart.

He sighed as he opened his correspondence, slicing open the first seal with the letter opener that his servants had placed next to him.

"From Ashford," he murmured, his brows rising as he read it.

"Well, I'll be," he said before placing it on the table, his first thought was that Percy would certainly be interested in the news. He supposed she would learn of it herself, however, as Ashford's sister was likely to write her.

"There you are," his uncle said as he walked into the room, surprising Noah, for at this hour he had usually already left to work at his bank.

"Here I am," Noah said. "Is all well?"

"All is just fine," his uncle said. "I wanted to talk to you about your time here."

"Oh?" Noah said warily, wondering if he had overstayed his welcome.

"Yes." His uncle nodded. "We have very much enjoyed having you in our home."

"Thank you," Noah replied. "I appreciate everything you have done for me."

"I was wondering how you are finding your work. Do you need any additional introductions?"

"You have been a great help, Uncle. I do appreciate all you have done in introducing me to so many families in Bath, and I have quite enjoyed my time here."

"I'm glad to hear it," his uncle replied, slapping him on the shoulder. "If you need an excuse to stay here so that you can continue courting the Holloway girl, however, just say the word and I can help."

"Lady Percy?" he said, pretending to be surprised. "I am not courting her."

"No?" His uncle sat back in his chair, taking a sip of his coffee. "You could have fooled me."

Noah shook his head. "I am not planning on marrying. At least, not a woman like Percy."

"Why not?" his uncle asked, raising a brow. "She's quite beautiful."

Noah chuckled without any humor. "That is part of the problem, Uncle. She is beautiful. She is from a well-connected family. She possesses a lovely countenance. And she likely comes with a very sizeable dowry, not that I am privy to such information. I am the last person she would be interested in marrying, and I am sure I'd be far from her father's first choice."

His uncle shook his head. "You are a good man, Noah. You should not think so little of yourself."

"I am only telling the truth."

"You are afraid to be hurt. That is the problem."

"I've been down this road before," Noah said. "I promised myself I would not return."

"What do you mean?"

"I mean that I thought I would marry before, until the woman offered herself to Eric instead."

"I see," his uncle said, furrowing his brow. "What did your brother do about it?"

"He didn't realize I had feelings for her. He flirted a bit but had no intentions for her himself. It was enough for me to realize, however, that I meant nothing to her, and likely never will to anyone else. I have nothing particularly interesting to offer."

"You have yourself."

Noah snorted. "What good is that?"

"You are too hard on yourself."

"I am realistic."

"So what is your plan, then? To spend your life alone?"

"I have friends. Family."

"But not love," his uncle said ruefully. "Well, son, I cannot tell you what to do or how to live your life. I can tell you, however, that you will regret not pursuing what you want – especially when it is so close."

"I've tried that before," Noah said, looking off in the distance. "I shall be fine without."

"Very well," his uncle said with a sigh as he rose from the table. "Whatever you say."

Noah nodded as he returned to his plate in front of him, even though he had lost most of his appetite.

"I shall see you tonight, Uncle," he said, and his uncle nodded before tipping back his cup to finish his coffee.

Noah would love to stay here in Bath, for many reasons. He could spend more time with Percy, perhaps – or at least find excuses to be in the same room as her from time to time – but he realized there was more at play. The thought of returning to London and truly beginning this great project was daunting. He was doubting himself once more, as he was so wont to do.

And, he decided, he was done with it. At least, in this aspect of his life.

"Thank you, Uncle," he said. "For everything, truly."

"Don't thank me yet," his uncle said, pushing away from the table. "Your aunt has a great deal of plans for you with some of the young women of Bath. You might have something else to say to me by the end of it."

He laughed at himself now as he walked away, and Noah put down his fork and followed him out. This was going to be an interesting day, indeed.

***

Percy was quite excited about the day ahead of her. From the moment she had heard they were to travel to Bath, she had imagined what it might be like to take in the waters.

Now she would finally know – even if she had to do so with her cousins' non-stop chattering excitedly in her ear.

"What do you think they will do? Do you think they will perfect my skin?" Rebecca asked, and Elizabeth smiled, clasping her hands together excitedly as they waited in the Pump Room for their water to be brought to them. They would drink them first before submerging themselves. Apparently, that was how the most benefit was found, and their aunt was quite keen on the healing she hoped it would bring to her muscles.

"Do you think they can act like a love potion, causing a man to fall in love with you?"

"Waters cannot do that, can they?"

"Why not? I've heard they can cure a barren womb."

"Then yes, you must be right," Rebecca said, before leaning in toward Elizabeth as they were served water in glasses. It was somewhat murky, with deposits floating around within it. "Do you have a certain gentleman in mind?"

Elizabeth shrugged coyly, her eyes taking on a twinkle. "Any will do, of course. While the most eligible man in Bath at the moment is Lord Stephen, Percy here has already claimed him."

"I have not *yet*," Percy chimed in with more conviction than she had meant to express, before shooting back the water in nearly one gulp, practically choking on the taste of it. "Ugh," she said as her cousins stared at her with wide eyes.

"What does it taste like?" Elizabeth asked.

"Like…" Percy wrinkled her nose as she sought a way to

describe it. "Water that an egg has been boiled in. With iron and salt added to it."

Elizabeth tilted her glass up to her lips and took a small sip, wrinkling her nose at it.

"It is not pleasant."

"No," Percy agreed.

"Think of your gentleman," Rebecca urged her, and Elizabeth took a breath and continued on her glass.

"So," Percy said nonchalantly – for really, the answer did not particularly matter, she was just making conversation– "which gentleman has caught your interest?"

"Actually, Percy, I wanted to speak to you about that," Elizabeth said, leaning in. "It is your friend, Mr. Rowley."

"Mr. Rowley?" she said, raising her eyebrows, annoyed at the twisting pain in her stomach at Elizabeth's revelation. "Why would you have any interest in him?"

"Well, he—"

She was interrupted, however, when their mothers joined them.

"Are you young ladies ready for the waters?" Percy's mother asked, looking between them, and Percy nodded resolutely. She had been looking forward to this part of it.

"We are."

"Come, then, time to change."

They led the three ladies out of the Pump Room, and before long they were dressed in their bathing garments, each a long cotton dress of dark colors, Percy's a midnight blue she particularly liked, even if the fabric was rather itching her skin.

"Why, this is lovely," Percy said when they reached the water of The Queen's Bath, where only women were allowed, starting down the stairs as the warmth of it wove its way into the fabric of her gown and caressed her skin.

They were surrounded by marble pillars and busts, and

she could see the attraction of spending time in such a place, even if her mother had secretly told her before they left that she had no belief that these waters actually worked any wonders – she had far more trust in the waters of the sea. But Percy's aunt was convinced, and so here they were.

Percy laughed as her cousins joined her and their heads bobbed above the water, as did the other ladies who dotted the small pool. Percy pushed herself backward as she stretched out her arms and feet, although the cotton dress considerably weighed her down.

She couldn't help that her mind continued to wander to Noah and Elizabeth's interest in him. She could hardly see anything in common between the two of them. Not that *she* and Noah were very similar and they did get on rather well, but still…

"Elizabeth," she said, paddling closer to her cousin, lowering her voice so that their mothers didn't hear, "what were you saying about Mr. Rowley?"

"Oh, only that his brother is an earl. I know I am not nearly high-born enough to capture an earl myself, but he is his brother, and you never know what could happen," she said, smiling dreamily.

"So you want him because he has the potential of becoming an earl one day?"

"Well, yes," Elizabeth said, her eyes wide that Percy would think to question such a thing. "Isn't that why anyone marries?"

She wasn't wrong, and yet somehow the thought of it caused a great deal of disturbance within Percy. She wanted to tell Elizabeth exactly what she thought, that she was using a good man who had far more depth to him besides his familial connections, but she knew if she questioned it, she would only bring attention to herself.

"Actually, Percy, if you could put in a good word…"

Percy stopped listening as her gaze was caught on a woman on the other side of the small pool. She recognized her. The dark hair, the heavily made-up face—then the woman turned and just about caught her eye. Mrs. MacNall. What was she doing here? Well, likely the same thing Percy was. She didn't want the woman to see her, didn't want her to question why they might be in the same location once more. She hoped that Mrs. MacNall wouldn't remember her, but she couldn't risk it, not with her nosy aunt and cousins nearby. So just before Mrs. MacNall spotted her, Percy did the only thing she could think of – she dunked herself under the water.

CHAPTER 20

"Why would you do such a thing?"

Her mother was staring at her from across the carriage, her expression incredulous as she stared at her now very soggy daughter. Percy had put herself to rights as best she could, though she was sorely missing her maid at the moment.

"It was an accident," Percy said, smiling weakly, as she attempted to comb her fingers through her hair.

"An accident," her mother repeated, clearly not believing her. "I do not know what to think sometimes, Persephone."

"I keep your life interesting," Percy said mischievously, and her mother did manage a slight laugh at that.

"That, you most certainly do," she said, shaking her head. "Were you hiding from someone?"

"No," Percy said quickly — perhaps a little too quickly.

"The Baths do draw all sorts of people," her mother said. "Why, I even saw a known mistress there."

"Did you now?" Percy said in a strangled voice. "How would you know the woman was a mistress?"

"Oh, Lord Chamberlain parades his Cyprian everywhere. It is so disrespectful to his wife."

Percy would have thought having a mistress at all was disrespectful, but she kept her mouth closed.

"I heard," her mother said, lowering her voice in a sure sign she was sharing gossip, even though there was no one else within the carriage to hear them, "that she dumped Chamberlain from her bed!"

"She did?" Percy asked, slightly interested now. Her mother was nodding enthusiastically.

"Yes. Something to do with him taking back a gift to give to another."

"Interesting," Percy said thoughtfully. So as much as their timing had seemed unfortunate, perhaps it had worked out in their favor, if it meant that Mrs. MacNall thought Lord Chamberlain had retrieved the necklace while he was in her chambers. She would have to tell Noah.

"Now, tell me," her mother said, "what is bothering you?"

"Nothing," Percy said, turning her face away, but her mother read her thoughts anyway.

"Persephone."

"Very well," she said with a sigh. "Elizabeth told me she is interested in Mr. Rowley. But only because of his connection to his brother and not because of who he is as a man."

Her mother leaned forward, staring at her. "Have you spoken to him yet?"

"No."

"You must," she said, patting her knee. "You do not want to have any regrets, and Lord Lecher is becoming increasingly persistent that you and Lord Stephen should have a future together."

"I know," she said, leaning back against the squabs. "I am trying to sort this out, Mother, truly I am."

"And you will," her mother said, before chuckling slightly,

lifting her hand to her mouth as though to stop the sound. "Although I am not sure you will catch any gentleman looking like that."

"Mother!" Percy said, her mouth dropping open in astonishment, but then she couldn't help herself – she began to laugh with her, and soon enough they were both laughing so hard they were unable to contain themselves – leading to a very astonished footman when he opened the carriage doors to the women once they arrived.

Percy knew she was lucky. Her mother believed in her to make the best decision for herself.

Now Percy just had to determine what that was.

* * *

Noah didn't see Percy again for another week – not until the news of the letter he had received came to pass.

He had just returned home from his work when he received a card from the butler. One that had arrived during the day.

Ashford, Covington, and the new Lady Covington, Ashford's sister, had arrived in Bath. And they were interested in seeing him – as well as Percy. They were so keen on following the next clue of this treasure hunt that they had not wanted to wait for them to travel to Castleton.

The card was inviting him to a dinner that evening, which likely meant that Lady Percy would also be in attendance.

He couldn't help but think about her the entirety of the day, and that evening, when he knocked on the door of the house that Ashford had rented, it was with a pounding in his chest.

Which was ridiculous, especially considering all they had been through and had experienced with one another.

"Rowley!" Covington greeted him with a wide grin and a

slap on his back after he was shown into the drawing room. Ashford, slightly more reserved than his closest friend, shook his hand.

"Thank you for coming," he said. "And thank you for all you have done for us."

"It's nothing, really," he mumbled, trying to stay present, but his eyes kept straying to the corner of the room where Percy and Lady Covington were sitting close to one another. Percy's back was to him, but she was talking animatedly, her hands moving fluidly through the air. He wondered if she was telling her friend about what had happened when they went to retrieve the necklace – and how much information she would impart.

He nearly walked over to join the conversation – something he would never even have considered a month ago – when someone else walked into the room, and his eyes widened at the presence.

"Eric?" he said when his brother hit him on the back enthusiastically. "What are you doing here?"

"I couldn't let my brother have all the fun!" Eric said with a laugh. He was everything that Noah wasn't – friendly, positive, the life of the room everywhere he went. The very reason why Leticia had chosen him. "When I heard that you had solved this thing – and had stolen back a necklace of all things – I couldn't help but come see if it was true."

"It is true."

They turned at the feminine voice to see that Percy and Lady Covington had walked over to join the larger conversation. Percy looked at Noah with a spark in her eyes.

"Mr. Rowley has become quite the adventurer."

"Who would have thought?" Eric said, his eyes narrowing slightly as he took in Noah. He paused.

"You look... different."

Noah shrugged, taking a sip of the scotch Ashford had passed him. "How so?"

"Your hair and face. Did you finally see fit to take some of the advice I've been offering you over the years?"

"I made a change," Noah muttered. "Nothing to get excited about."

"It was part of our mission," Percy said. "He had to charm a woman."

"Did you, now?" Eric said, suddenly quite intrigued, and Noah wished that Percy hadn't said anything. He and his brother may be the best of friends, but they were still brothers, which meant that Eric loved to learn anything he could to irk Noah. "How did you manage?"

"Fine," Noah said, shooting Percy a look, hoping she would understand that she should change the subject.

"More than fine," she said, either not picking up on what he was trying to tell her or continuing regardless. "He was invited to the woman's home."

"Do tell us more," Eric said, leaning in.

"Nothing happened," Noah said, waving a hand away. "I stopped it."

"Why?"

"Because it... wasn't right," he said, even though that was far from the truth.

"As entertaining as this conversation might be, why do we not go into dinner and discuss more about the actual clue that you discovered?" Ashford said, mercifully putting an end to the conversation, which lacked all levels of appropriateness.

They followed him in, taking a seat around the table as the footmen served the first course. Noah found himself seated next to Percy, and he wasn't sure if he was glad of it or not.

"So," Ashford said as they all took their first taste of the turtle soup, which was so terrible that Noah wondered if they had brought their cook from Castleton. "The necklace did contain a clue?"

"Yes," Noah said, glad they were back to speaking about facts and not his part in this entire story. "A small piece of paper, with two words on it – *San Sebastian*."

Ashford and his sister exchanged a glance.

"Are you certain?" Ashford asked, putting down his spoon, and Noah nodded.

"Yes, but we were uncertain of what it meant."

"San Sebastian is on the north coast of Spain and is where our grandmother is from," Lady Covington said. "Our grandfather travelled there and that is where they met."

"So what do you think it means?" Percy asked, leaning forward excitedly. "Do you think that is where the treasure could be?"

"Or, more likely, the next clue," Ashford said with a sigh, clearly growing tired of this never-ending chase that could very likely end with nothing. "Whoever planned this hunt certainly didn't make it easy."

"Perhaps that is the point," Noah said, rubbing his chin, still surprised to find it bare. "Could it be that only someone determined and intelligent enough should be able to find it?"

"Perhaps," Ashford said with a tilt of his head. "I suppose there is nothing to be done now but travel there and see what we can find."

"Will you go, Gideon?" his sister asked, and he sighed.

"I'd like to, but I have too many pressing matters at home," he said. "I do not think I could leave, as I have far too much to look after. I do not want to leave and risk anything occurring with Father."

"Fair enough," Lady Covington said.

"The two of you could go," Ashford said, and the husband and wife exchanged a glance.

"I do not think we can," Lady Covington said, an odd expression on her face.

"Why not?"

"Well..." she said slowly, and Percy suddenly grinned at her.

"You are with child, aren't you?" Percy said, excitement in her voice, and Lady Covington laughed.

"We are! I can hardly believe it."

"That is amazing," Percy said. "Congratulations."

They all added their well wishes, Noah's leg brushing against Percy's when he leaned forward. He could sense her cognizance of him, but he had been aware of her presence from the moment she had sat down, so it was nothing new to him.

After a time, the topic returned to the matter at hand.

"What should we do about chasing after this next clue?" Lady Covington asked.

"I will go to Spain," Eric said, surprising them all.

"You will?" Noah asked with a raised brow.

"Sure," Eric said with a shrug. "I have nothing else to do and I feel I haven't been of much help in this venture so far. It's been a time since we have all done anything daring together, has it not?"

"I would be ever so grateful," Ashford said, but Eric waved a hand at him.

"I have never been to Spain, and I would certainly enjoy the opportunity," he said with a grin, and Noah didn't miss how Percy turned to him with a wide smile on her face. He hated how jealous he was at just that bit of attention from her. He could volunteer himself, but he had to return to London and had made promises to various families who had offered them their homes. Besides, it shouldn't matter so much what she thought of him. Why was she turning him into such a fool?

Then there was the fact he didn't agree this was the best decision.

"Are you certain this is the best decision?" Noah asked. "Spaniards will be suspicious of an Englishman, never mind that the French are currently unpredictable."

"I speak Spanish," Eric said. "I will pass myself off as a local."

"Still," Noah said, uncertain, "there is the travel, and—"

"Noah," Eric said, stopping him, although not unkindly. "This is why I volunteered and not you. This excites me, not scares me."

"Tell me, Lord Ferrington," Percy said in the silence as the third course arrived. "What do you do to keep entertained most days?"

Eric launched into answering her question, clearly excited about doing so, as Noah sat there silently fuming, though unable to do anything about it.

He had seen this play before. This was the beginning of the second act, and he knew where it would end – with the woman wanting another, another beside him, and most likely his brother.

His feelings for this woman were becoming far too strong.

It was only going to lead to a broken heart.

Again.

CHAPTER 21

*P*ercy could sense that Noah was becoming increasingly frustrated, but she had no idea why. She appreciated the opportunity to learn more about his brother, mostly because Lord Ferrington was important to Noah and she was interested in the contrast between them.

But Noah didn't seem so pleased about their conversation. Perhaps he was worried that she might learn something about him that she wouldn't like?

She hadn't seen him for an entire week, and the truth was, she missed him, but she hadn't been able to come up with any reason as to why they should spend time together. They had retrieved the necklace and found the clue within – why else would she need to see him?

Because she wanted him. That was the truth.

She had been unable to stop thinking of their kisses, as well as what they had shared. He had shown her things, taught her things that she would like to repeat. She wasn't sure what kind of woman that made her, but he had awakened something within her that she hadn't been able to put back to sleep.

The strangest part of it was that it wasn't just what they had done. It was him. When she imagined anyone else – not just Lord Stephen but *any* other man – doing the same with her, she was unaffected. It was Noah himself.

Even sitting next to him at dinner was causing all sorts of ideas to stroll through her mind. Sensing his increasing unease, she reached out, placing her hand on his thigh. He started slightly but didn't look at her, and showed no other outward sign.

But nor did he remove her hand.

She started inching it up higher, his only reaction the tightening of his jaw.

Then she brushed her fingers over what was becoming an increasingly large bulge in his breeches.

He visibly jumped now, a slight sheen of perspiration breaking out over his forehead.

He shook his head slightly.

She smiled, continuing to try to placate him.

He swallowed hard.

She nudged her knee against his.

He wrapped his hand around hers in an apparent half-hearted attempt to force her to stop.

She continued.

"Noah?"

His brother was staring at him from across the table.

"Are you all right? You look… flushed."

"Fine," Noah said, clearing his throat and reaching for his wine glass. "Just fine."

"You sound strained. Are you choking?"

"Just a bit of something in my throat." Noah took a large sip of his drink.

"Apologies," Ashford said from the head of the table. "The cook came highly recommended, but perhaps there was something wrong with a bit of the meat. I shall make a complaint."

"No, please do not on my account," Noah said, waving a hand in the air, and Percy took pity on him and pulled her hand away. "It was just an error on my part. All is fine."

An error? Was he calling her a mistake?

The rest of the dinner passed without any additional mishap, and soon enough the ladies rose to retire. Percy would have rather that they all stay together, but the gentlemen promised they would join them soon.

The ladies were heading into the drawing room when Percy saw Noah leave the room behind them, heading down the corridor to what appeared to be garden doors. She took one step into the drawing room, made her excuses for a brief respite, and then followed him out. When she pushed through the doors into the refreshingly cool night air, it took her a moment to find Noah.

"Where are you?" she murmured until she found him on the bench overlooking the small back mews.

"Noah?" she whispered into the night, and he started before turning around to look at her.

"Percy, what are you doing?" he asked, his voice laced with tension.

"I came to see if all was well."

"It is not. Thanks to you," he said gruffly, and she couldn't help but laugh, even though guilt tugged at her for being the cause of his current situation.

"My apologies," she said, sinking down next to him on the bench. "It appears that I had too much fun with the situation."

"So it seems."

"I truly am sorry," she said, leaning into him and looking up at him from beneath her lashes. "Can I make it up to you?"

"How do you suggest doing that?"

"I can think of ways," she said, her fingers crawling along his waistband, but he playfully swatted her hand away.

"That is how we got to this place."

"Yes, but this time I could finish it."

He turned his head from one side to the other. "We are in the middle of a garden."

"Yes."

"In a public place."

"Yes."

"Anyone could come back here."

"I still have not heard any objection."

He sat up, taking her hands in his.

"You would be ruined if we were discovered in such a position. As you would even if we were merely found back here alone, if we are being honest."

"Then why do we not do something to make it worthwhile?"

He closed his eyes and his lips moved as though he was saying a prayer.

"Noah," she whispered, leaning toward him. "I want you. All of you."

"You are an innocent young woman," he said, but his lips were nearly pressed together.

"Who wishes to be innocent no more," she continued playfully, her hands pressing against his thighs. "Please?"

He let out a sigh as he opened his eyes. "Not here."

Her heart leaped. "Somewhere else?"

"We shouldn't."

"But?"

"My aunt and uncle are out at an event tonight. If you wish to... further things, I suppose we could sneak you into the house."

She clapped her hands together in glee before she realized she was making herself look like a young fool. "Wonderful," she said. "I shall come to the back door, then?"

He shot her a stern look. "I will come to you and walk you to the house."

"But—"

He shook his head. "You will not be walking the streets of Bath alone. Especially in the late hours."

"I have done it before."

"That was foolhardy."

She raised a brow elegantly. "I do hope you are not calling me a fool."

"I said your actions were foolhardy. But then, who am I to talk when I am agreeing to this with you?"

"It will be fun," she said with a grin. "You'll see."

"That's what I'm afraid of," she heard him murmur as she stood and walked away, their banter adding a lightness to her step.

* * *

Noah was the fool now.

He and Percy were walking together in charged silence to his aunt and uncle's home. After the party had retired for the evening, he had returned there alone as expected. Eric had wanted to continue the party elsewhere, and Noah had been glad when he went out on his own after Noah made an excuse of needing to retire early for the night.

Eric was disappointed, but it didn't seem to bother him to continue the evening's entertainment without Noah.

Percy had been waiting for him with an eager grin on her face, and Noah found that he couldn't turn her down. Not only did he not have it within him to do so, but he was concerned that she would assume there was something wrong with her if he said no.

Which was so far from the truth. He supposed now he would have to show her just how far.

The air of anticipation between them, one that appeared to be near to crackling, had happened the moment she had slipped out the door of her house clad in a navy cloak. They both appeared to be anticipating what was to come, and Noah wondered how, once they were finished with one another, anything could ever be the same again.

He opened the back door, entering first so that he could look from one side to the next to determine if any of the servants were still about. He had given his valet the night off and assumed that just his aunt's lady's maid and uncle's valet would be waiting for their master and mistress to return. Finding no one about, he waved Percy in, and she remained close to him as they hurried up the stairs to his bedroom. When he shut the door behind them, he nearly sagged against it with relief.

Meanwhile, Percy was near to giddy as she all but pounced upon him, her fingers drifting up his chest.

"We made it," she said with a rush of glee.

"We did."

"Does it not make it so much more exciting with the knowledge that we could be caught?"

No, it certainly did not. "I suppose."

She pushed him backwards until his shoulders hit the door behind him.

"I missed you this week," she said, and he wondered how a woman as vibrant as she could miss a man as boring as he in her life. He stared into her eyes to find that she wasn't lying, her pupils large and dark.

"I missed you too," he said thickly, stroking his hands over her hair and down her arms.

"Do you think about what we did together?" she asked, her hands encircling his neck.

THE SCHOLAR'S KEY

"Every day. Every night," he said as she removed his spectacles, and he appreciated when she placed them gently on the table beside the bed.

"I haven't been able to stop thinking about it," she said, leaning into him, and Noah paused, for just a moment. Obviously, it had been her first time doing anything of such a nature, and he had awakened something within her. But he knew better than to think it had anything to do with him, but rather *what* he had shown her.

He should stop now, should make sure she saved herself for her husband.

Then she stood on her toes and pressed her lips against his.

And he didn't seem to have any ability to say no.

CHAPTER 22

*I*t was like spilling oil on a kitchen fire. All that had been simmering, slowly burning, combusted, destroying along with it all of Noah's reservations. All of the hesitation that Percy had sensed there before seemed to disappear, as his hands wrapped around her hips and lifted her onto the high bed. His arms came around her, holding her close against him, as though he wanted to keep her pressed up against him forever.

Which, at the moment, Percy would be more than happy with.

The kiss, which had seemed to already be laced with more passion than Percy could have imagined, turned even deeper, more desperate, as their tongues battled and their lips plundered.

Noah laid her back on the bed, Percy crying out when his lips left hers, but then she forgave him when it was only for his tongue to trail along her jaw, stopping to nip at her ear before he continued down her neck. Percy writhed beneath him, needing more while also enjoying all that he was doing to her.

Her every nerve was so heightened that she wondered how she was ever going to survive this.

But she was more than eager to find out.

His generous mouth sucked at her collarbone, then travelled down her chest, his lips brushing over her nipple through the thin layer of the drab dress she had worn for this liaison. She couldn't stop the whimper that emerged from her throat as she arched her breasts toward him, wanting more.

He acquiesced, although not in the way she had been guessing. He reached around her, loosening the large buttons of her gown before tugging it down over her shoulders, and she helped him, pushing the sleeves off her arms.

Once he removed the trappings of her chemise, he leaned back, sitting on his knees as he stared at her, his eyes wide.

"Percy, you are so beautiful," he said reverently, before leaning down and raining kisses all over her breasts.

She smiled as she took his head in her hands, wishing that he would put his mouth on her nipple, as he was so close to it, yet so far. She wondered if he was leaving it alone now on purpose.

"You are better than my dreams," he breathed while licking a circle around one nipple, her back arching as he blew on it.

"You dream of me?" she whimpered, and he looked up at her, smiling wickedly.

"Every night."

He didn't appear to be needing a response, but she couldn't help her need any longer.

"Noah?"

"Yes?"

"Please, will you… will you…"

She didn't know how to say what she wanted, but he seemed to understand.

"Yes. Of course."

He took her nipple in his mouth once more, and Percy cried out at the incredible sensation that began at her nipple and then soared through her entire body. He moved to her other breast while his fingers came to appease the one he was leaving behind.

She held his head in place, not wanting this to end, but he didn't seem to hear her thoughts as suddenly he was abandoning her – until she realized that he was only doing so to take his jacket and shirt off. That, she was absolutely fine with, for she wanted to see more.

Percy had no expectations of what might happen after this. They hadn't spoken of the future, and as far as she was aware, Noah had no interest in a wife – or at least, in *her* as a wife – but then, she didn't want to think of that right now.

This, their coming together, felt like it had been building for so long that it was nearly unavoidable. And she knew that this was no time for words, that their bodies were doing the talking.

Noah returned to her, and she couldn't help her groan of relief, as she arched her hips and sought out his, not entirely knowing what she was doing, but acting on instinct.

Her knowledge, at least, was expansive, more than most innocent young ladies, between the scandalous books she and her friends read, and then the whispered explanations of her two married friends.

She was both excited and terrified.

Noah leaned down, kissing her once more, until he finally pulled away, his eyes searching hers. His were nearly glazed over in apparent need of her, their hazel irises seemingly piercing through her soul.

"I'll try to go slow."

"Don't," she said fiercely, as she reached down to find the fall of his breeches, helping him slide them down his legs.

Percy leaned up on her elbows, taking in her fill of the sight of him again. His cock, standing at attention, seemed bigger than before, if that was at all possible.

It was ready for her.

He gently spread her legs apart, and while she certainly felt not only vulnerable at being so exposed again but also nervous as to what was to come, she trusted him so implicitly that her fears were eased by the knowledge that he would take care of her.

Noah brought his thumb to her bundle of nerves as he slipped a finger inside. Percy was embarrassed at just how wet she was, waiting for him, but he didn't seem to mind as the corners of his mouth curled upward in satisfaction.

"Percy, are you sure?" he asked, his voice husky. "Say the word and we'll stop. Or swivel."

She searched his face, and while it was full of thick tension at what she was sure he needed, she appreciated that he was willing to do as she pleased. He had started this for her, and he would stop this for her too – if she chose.

"I am," she said, finding that she was hardly able to say the words aloud, so clogged her throat was with emotion. "Are you?"

"Against my better judgement..." he said taking in a jagged breath, "absolutely."

He leaned in, placing a soft kiss on her lips.

"I trust you, Noah," she said into his mouth. "Show me what it feels like to make love."

He nodded, pressing his forehead against hers, and now it wasn't tension between them but rather emotion – scaring her at how firmly she was in its grip.

Noah's body covered hers, one of his hands splaying across her hip to hold her steady. Percy reached up, gripping the wiry muscles of his forearms as she waited for him.

He lifted his head just enough that he was looking into

her eyes, and, keeping them locked together, he notched the head of his cock into her, moving ever so slowly. Percy's eyes widened in shock at the feel of him inside, at how he stretched her.

"Stop," she said, and he did exactly as she said, but when he began to pull out of her, she shook her head, her arms climbing to his biceps to keep him where he was. "I just need a moment," she said, slightly panting. "But do not go anywhere."

He nodded, waiting, and finally, Percy relaxed again, adjusting to his girth.

"I'm ready," she said, smiling at his worried expression, and she had to wrap her legs around his back and pull him forward into her to convince him to move again.

He closed his eyes as he sank forward into her. "Percy," he groaned as she reached her arms around him, holding him as close as she could.

He thrust his hips forward, then back out again, moving deeper into her each time. No longer uncomfortable, Percy whimpered at the sensations that filled her. Her books had not quite prepared her for what this would feel like.

Noah reached down, caressing her again, and Percy nearly shot off the bed as pure pleasure filled her. Her legs still wrapped around him, she urged him on with her heels, and he matched her thrust for thrust.

"Noah," she heard echo in the air around her, a pleading edge to it, and it took a moment to realize it was coming from her own mouth.

Before she knew it, the sweet promise of release began to make itself known, as her every sense turned toward Noah. When he bent his head and sucked hard on one of her nipples, Percy lost all control as her world exploded into pieces. It was only just starting to come back together when

Noah pulled himself out of her before finishing on the sheet next to her.

When he was done, he turned to her, pulling her close to his side as he sighed contentedly into her neck.

"Percy," he mumbled as he nuzzled her, "Nothing... no one... has ever felt so right before."

"Will you hold me for a while?" she asked, hating the tremor in her voice, but after what they had just experienced together, she felt a need to be close to him, to know that this had some meaning – for she knew, no matter what happened in her life, she would never forget this.

"Always," he said, his voice rumbling underneath her ear as she lay her head on his hard chest.

"Do you mean that?" she asked, hating her vulnerability and how much she had come to depend on it.

He stroked a hand over her hair. "Anytime you need anything, Percy, you know that I will be there for you."

She nodded, knowing the truth in that, even as she wondered in what way he was referring. "Thank you."

She wasn't sure how long they lay together, but at some point, she must have dozed off, for the next thing she knew, Noah was gently shaking her shoulder.

"Percy," he whispered in her ear, "the sun is beginning to rise."

"What?" She bolted upright and glanced out the window. "Oh, no."

"We best get you home before anyone is awake to see you."

"I cannot believe I slept this long."

But, oh, it had felt so right to be curled up in Noah's arms. He might not have as broad of shoulders and as wide of thighs as she had imagined her man to have, but he was deceptively attractive and had greater character than any man she had ever met.

Now was the time to tell him how she felt – and see if he returned her affection.

"Noah—"

"Don't."

She frowned at him as she stood and began to dress.

"You do not even know what I am going to say."

"I have an idea," he said, rising himself and beginning to pull on his clothes with more aggression than she would have thought he had within him. "You feel that, in this moment, we have a closeness, a tenderness, and you were going to say something about your emotion toward me. Am I right?"

"I suppose you are, yes." She swallowed hard, not liking where this was going.

"It is just the moment, Percy. We shared an intimacy as close as two people can get. You will return home and soon enough you will remember this with fondness and nothing more."

Percy had to bite her tongue to keep from lashing out. As it was, she didn't hold back. Who was this man? Where was the gentleman who had made love to her and then held her so tenderly? "How dare you tell me what I feel?"

"Both of us should know the truth," he said, and she realized then the problem – he was protecting himself.

"Do you think that you do not mean anything to me?"

He didn't respond as he stepped behind her and began to fasten her dress. She didn't protest as she had no other way of dressing, but she had been too proud to ask him during an argument.

"I know that I mean something to you," he said quietly. "But soon enough someone else – someone better – will come along and you will be glad that you have not further attached yourself to me."

"How can you say that?"

"I know it to be true."

The expression on his face was one of such conviction that she knew he fully believed in what he was saying.

"Did something like this happen to you before?"

He averted his gaze. "We need to go."

She allowed him to sneak her out of the house and walk her back to her own, keeping her hood low over her face so that no one would recognize her. She was rather shocked by the number of people who were out and working already at such an early hour.

They arrived at the back door of her townhouse, and Noah turned, as though ready to leave – but she wasn't going to allow him to do so that easily.

She stood her ground in front of him, placing a hand on his chest. "Noah."

"Percy, you—"

"It is imperative that you tell me the truth right now."

He waited as she tried to find the words she needed.

"Our night together was… so wonderful and I will treasure it forever. You have shown me more than I ever thought possible, and I am so grateful. This morning, however, has been unexpected. I must know… do you feel anything for me? Do you feel enough to… well, to consider starting a life with me?"

She held her breath, hating the racing of her heart, but her entire future rested on his answer.

He blinked. "Do you mean marriage?"

"Yes."

"I—"

Before he could respond, however, the door flew open, revealing her mother standing at the entrance.

"Persephone Holloway, just what do you think you are doing?"

CHAPTER 23

Noah froze as though he was a schoolboy who had been caught with his hand in the pudding.

"Mother!" Percy managed to reply so cheerfully he wondered if she realized the severity of their current situation.

"Do you know what time it is?" her mother said. "One of the maids went in to stoke the fire in your room and imagine her surprise when you were nowhere to be found! She woke your lady's maid, who told my lady's maid, who told the housekeeper, who—"

"I get the idea," Percy said dryly. "It went up the servant gossip chain until someone told you and now the entire house knows."

"Yes, you could say that."

Percy sighed, rubbing her forehead. "May I have a moment to finish my conversation with Noah?"

Her mother looked at her and then back at Noah as though they had lost their minds – which Noah in turn wondered if she had.

"It is six o'clock in the morning and you have been out all

night with a man who is not your family, while meanwhile you are betrothed to someone else!"

Noah felt all the blood drain from his head as Percy's mouth dropped open.

"Mother—"

"You are betrothed?" he asked, keeping his voice emotionless.

She shook her head from one side to the next, looking at Noah beseechingly. "It's not like that. I have not agreed to anything."

"I do not know if you will have the option anymore," her mother said with a quiet steeliness. "After this debacle, I am not sure if the man will still have you."

"Good. Then I do not have to turn him down," Percy said triumphantly, and Noah took a breath.

"Is it Lord Stephen?" he asked.

"Yes," Percy's mother responded for her. "It is. Now, Persephone, I suggest you come inside before the servants from all the houses on this street see you out here and your name is on the lips of *all* the gossips tomorrow. We have much to discuss. Good day, Mr. Rowley."

Percy stepped forward with her mother but turned to Noah. "Will you call on me?"

He shook his head slowly, the triumphant haze of the night dissipating as reality began to settle in once more. "I do not think that is wise."

"Noah—"

But her mother shut the door before she could finish, leaving him standing out in the mews alone until he began the walk home.

He wasn't sure what she had wanted him to say, but the truth was, she was better off with a man like Lord Stephen – even if she didn't realize it yet.

*　*　*

"And then he *what?*" Cassandra listened to her tale with rapt attention. Percy was sitting next to her on the sofa, her voice low as she whispered her story. When she was finished, Cassandra sat back, blinking. Percy knew her friend wouldn't have been shocked by her indiscretion – if anyone could understand, it would be Cassandra – but likely, rather by the part Noah had played through the story.

"I don't understand," Cassandra said, waving away the pastry tray when a maid brought it in and placed it in front of them, her face turning rather green. "Why would he not say anything? Or offer for you? I do not believe Mr. Rowley is a man who frequently beds various women – one would think it would mean something for him to do so. Besides, I have seen the way he looks at you."

"Like what?"

"Like he loves you."

"He does not!" Percy practically yelled, which only made Cassandra grin even wider.

"Do you love him?'

"I—I enjoy his company. I long for his touch. I feel safe with him. I know that he will take care of me and never allow any harm to come to me. I don't feel that with Lord Stephen, but nor do I feel excitement with Lord Stephen either. The risk with him is not worth the potential reward. Lord Stephen... he makes my skin crawl, to be honest."

"What does that tell you?"

Percy sighed. "I would like to get to know Noah better. But I need to answer my father tomorrow, and meanwhile, Noah will not even speak to me. While I am not sure if he loves me, I do have the feeling that he cares for me. Something is holding him back."

Cassandra pursed her lips. "I think I know what it might be."

"You do?"

"You cannot tell him that I told you. I only know because Devon told me, and I shouldn't be breaking his trust. But I can see that you think this is about you and I need you to know it is not."

"Very well," Percy said, slightly uneasy that she could be causing controversy between Cassandra and her husband, but she couldn't help the clawing need to know more about Noah's past.

"Noah was all but betrothed to a woman. He did all as was proper. He courted her, spoke to her father, and considered their marriage all but complete."

"But?"

Cassandra winced. "But then she met his brother, Eric, and realized just how handsome and single he was. She decided that he was the better brother."

Percy gasped. "He took his brother's intended?"

Cassandra shook her head. "Not purposely. Eric had been away and hadn't realized that she and Mr. Rowley had an understanding. As soon as they met, they began a flirtation – although once he learned the truth, he put a stop to it immediately, of course. However, it would explain why Noah doesn't believe that you would be interested in him over another."

Percy wrinkled her nose. "Why would he think I would do the same as this woman?"

Cassandra shrugged. "Why wouldn't he? It was what he knew to be true in the past so he likely has no cause to think it would be any different this time. Also, while Mr. Rowley is a pleasant man in all ways, he does not exactly stand out, nor does he have a title to attract women. Have you given him reason to think that you might choose him over another?"

Percy considered her actions with him the night before — even as she bristled at Cassandra's description of Noah, though she could see why Cassandra might believe what she did. One didn't see the true side of Noah until looking closer.

But in answer to Cassandra's question, certainly, Noah must know that she would never give herself to a man if she had no intention of pursuing anything further with him – wouldn't he?

"I told him that I cared for him," she said. "I even asked if he had any thoughts about a future with me."

"And then?"

"And then my mother interrupted and informed him that I was betrothed to Lord Stephen."

Cassandra blinked. "You are betrothed to Lord Stephen?"

"No," Percy said but then winced. "Not entirely. Not yet."

"Oh dear," Cassandra said with a sigh. "I think you need a brandy. And then you need to figure out just what you are going to do with your life."

"I was afraid you were going to say that," Percy said, but she accepted the drink and finished it with a flourish.

"There is something else I should tell you," Cassandra said, her expression uneasy, and Percy had a feeling that there was more to it than her usual stomach upset.

"What is it?"

"We visited my Aunt Eve a couple of days ago."

"How is she doing? She is an intriguing woman. I quite enjoyed her."

"She is," Cassandra said with a large smile before it fell. "Her necklace was stolen again."

"What?" Percy gasped.

"She has no idea how," Cassandra said, waving her hands in the air. "She said she put it back in its case and hid the key elsewhere. Yet somehow, it was stolen, without any harm to the case."

"Noah was right," Percy murmured.

"What do you mean?"

"He said that it was important we determine how the necklace was stolen in the first place. Meanwhile, I was simply happy that we had been able to return it."

"At least you were able to solve the clue."

"Yes, but the necklace meant so much to your aunt," Percy said. "I hate to think that she no longer has it."

Cassandra patted her knee. "Well, hopefully in time we will find it."

"Did anyone else know where the key was?"

"Not that Aunt Eve was aware."

"Well, I am sorry, Cassandra. I will keep my eye out. And," a slight hope filled her chest at the thought of having a reason to see Noah again, "perhaps I can speak to Noah about asking the woman who had it before if she has seen it again."

"Perhaps," Cassandra said, obviously forcing a smile for Percy's sake. "Or you could just tell him what you'd like to speak about."

Percy groaned. "You know me too well."

"Not too well," Cassandra said with a smile. "Perhaps just well enough."

* * *

THERE WAS nothing left for Noah in Bath.

He had researched as much as he could and had made copies and notes for what appeared to be most important. He had found the necklace and solved the clue. And he had learned that Percy was going to marry another.

He didn't know why it had come as such a surprise. He had always known that he could not be the man for her.

She was a woman who enjoyed life, took risks, and

yearned for excitement and adventure. He was boring, staid, and would rather see the world through books than see it himself firsthand.

Even so, somehow, learning that she was already promised to be married while she spent the night with him felt like taking a punch to the gut.

"Where are you going?"

He looked up to see his brother standing in the doorway, and a sense of guilt filled his chest. "I'm sorry, Eric. I know you just arrived, but I am going to return to London."

"Already?"

"Yes."

"Why?" Eric asked, bewildered. "I thought you were here for another week, at least."

"Circumstances have changed," he said, "and I am looking forward to actually doing something with my life."

"You have done a great deal already."

"Like what?" Noah asked with a snort. "I do not think I am of much value to anyone."

"I am not sure how you could say that. I could not ask for a better friend, let alone a brother. You are a dutiful son, you strive to do right by others, you are loyal to a fault."

"I appreciate all of that, Eric, truly I do, but please understand, I need to leave."

"Is this about Lady Percy?" Eric asked, and when Noah fixed his stare on him, his brother had a knowing look on his face, an eyebrow raised.

"Maybe," Noah said with a sigh, giving up the pretense, before sitting heavily on the bed. "Despite my better judgement, Eric, I have fallen for her. But she and I are not meant to be. I am not what she needs – nor what she wants. Not as a husband."

"How do you know this?"

"At Whitehall's wedding, I overheard her speaking to her

mother. She wants a man with strength, both physically and forcefully. A man who can give her all of the excitement that she is looking for. I am not that man. But Lord Stephen is."

"Lord Stephen?"

"The man she is apparently betrothed to. Who she never told me about."

"I see," Eric said, rubbing his thumb over his chin. "And does she know how you feel?"

"Not entirely."

"What does *she* feel for you?"

Noah rubbed a hand over the back of his neck. "I don't know for certain…"

"But…"

"But I have reason to believe that she, at least, feels some affection for me. But I do not believe it stretches any further than that. Certainly not to a lifetime together."

"Have you asked her?"

"No!"

"Why not?"

"I've been down that path before, Eric," Noah said with a curse. "I do not wish to take it again."

"You do know how sorry I am for what happened with Leticia?" Eric asked quietly.

"I know. You have told me often enough. But in the end, you did me a favor, for I learned the truth about her before it was too late."

Eric was silent, and Noah knew he was trying to find a way to argue with him, but finally, he pushed away from the doorframe. "Will you promise me something?"

Noah crossed his arms but didn't yet agree.

"Do not go to London yet. I am to return to Castleton with Ashford shortly. Will you come with us for a short time?"

"Why?"

"Because you are good company. Because I feel that you need some levity right now. And because I should like you to see me off before I travel to Spain."

"Are you truly going to do that?"

"Of course." Eric grinned. "It's the adventure that I've always dreamed about – even if you do not understand it yourself. Now, take a day or two to say your farewells to our aunt and uncle, allow them to understand how grateful you are for all that they have done for you, and then we shall leave for Castleton together. How does that sound?"

"I suppose it sounds all right."

"Good," Eric said with a smile. "It will all turn out as it should, Noah. You will see."

Somehow, Noah didn't quite believe him.

CHAPTER 24

Noah couldn't stop thinking about Percy.

Which was why, despite his better judgment, he agreed to see her just one last time before he left Bath – and all of the memories it held.

He wasn't sure how to make it happen but was pleased when Ashford agreed to arrange their meeting, for no one would question Percy wanting to spend time with her friend, Lady Covington.

Noah was making his way through Milsom Street when a figure ahead of him made him stop directly where he stood in the middle of the busy street.

When he realized the identity of the woman walking closer toward him, he wanted to turn around and run the other way.

But it was too late. She had seen him.

"Noah! How are you?"

He took a deep breath, stepping to the side of the pavement to allow pedestrians to pass by while he made his greetings.

"Lady Turner. I am well. How are you?" he said, showing no signs of the familiarity she was bestowing upon him.

"I am fine. It is so good to see you," she said, a slight smile on her lips. "It has been so long."

"So it has."

"What has happened since…"

"Since you married?" he finished for her, raising a brow. He looked around her to see that she was alone, but for a maid who was following behind with what appeared to be purchases. Leticia had always enjoyed the finer things in life – hence, why she had married someone with much more title and wealth after Eric had turned her down.

"I am researching and writing," he said, desperate to finish this conversation. It was so strange seeing her again. He had remembered her and their relationship as so much more heightened. And yet now, seeing her, he felt… nothing. It was more so that he was already on edge about his upcoming conversation with Percy – one in which he was going to tell her goodbye. He didn't need this now. It was an inconvenience over anything else.

"I see," she said, not quite masking the grimace which he knew was because he was working. "And have you married?"

"No."

Her face fell, and it was then he realized that she did, at least, feel some guilt at what she had done to him.

"How is Lord Turner?" he asked, doing his utmost to be polite.

"Fine."

The conversation was stilted, and as Noah stared into the face of the woman he had thought he loved, a realization settled upon him – he had never loved her. Not like he had loved Percy. Letitia – Lady Turner – was beautiful, yes, but beauty faded in time and that was not what drew Noah to Percy. It was her spirit, her joy for life, her ability to love everyone around her. Which was why it would hurt so much more when she left him than it had when Letitia had done the same.

"I best be going now," he said, tipping his hat toward her. "Goodbye, Lady Turner."

"Goodbye, Noah," she said. "I wish you the best."

He had taken two steps when she called out to him, and he turned around.

"Yes?"

"I truly am sorry — for everything. You are a good man and I hope you find love one day. In the end, Noah, we were not right for one another. That was why I left you. Not for any other reason."

He didn't want to hear it. Somehow it made it all the worse that she left him because of who he was and not because of his lack of title or wealth.

He turned around and continued, leaving his past behind him.

* * *

Percy paced the foyer of the home that Lord Ashford had rented in Bath. Cassandra and her husband were also staying here, even though she was sure they could have afforded two places. But Lord Ashford and Lord Covington were as close as brothers, so she supposed it made sense.

She tried to tell herself that she was only looking out the window to see what weather the day had brought, even though she knew she was lying to herself – she was watching for Noah, on edge as to what he wanted to speak to her about.

As much as a small piece of her hoped against all odds that he was coming to tell her that he loved her, that he wanted to marry her and begin a life together, the practical side of her knew better.

Which meant she was just going to have to convince him of the truth.

She continued to pace as the longcase clock ticked the seconds away, leaving her to wonder just what was keeping Noah, who was always punctual to a fault. Finally, she caught sight of him, recognizing his steady, purposeful gait, and she hurried away from the window so fast she nearly tripped over her skirts before he could see her watching for him.

His knock sounded, and Percy waited for the butler to show him in. She knew, the moment he stepped through the drawing room door, from the lines etched into his forehead and the grim set of his lips, that she was not going to be pleased with his approach to the conversation.

"Percy," he greeted her in a low voice, and as he shut the door behind him, Percy decided that she wasn't going to allow him to break this off with her – not without her protest. She took a few strides toward him, wrapped her arms around his neck, and pulled him close. He hesitated before his arms came around her, returning her embrace.

"I missed you," she whispered into his neck, and she felt his arms tighten around her.

"I missed you too," he said gruffly, and when she tilted her head up to kiss him, he only gave her a quick press of his lips before he stepped back and set her away from him.

"Noah, I need to explain."

"There is no need."

"But there is," she insisted, searching his eyes. "I am not engaged. My father and Lord Stephen's father arranged this without consulting me. I only found out the day that we – that we came together. I never agreed to the marriage."

"Then why did your mother say you are betrothed?"

She dropped her eyes, knowing that the answer would be damning, but she wasn't going to lie.

"I told them that I needed time to decide."

"I see."

She lifted her eyes to his. "I needed time because I first had to ask if *you* felt anything toward me. It is you I want, Noah. Not Lord Stephen, nor anyone else for that matter. I never would have come to your bed if it was otherwise."

She saw a glimmer of hope in his eyes, but then it quickly disappeared.

"You would tire of me."

"Why would you say that?"

"You have no wish for a man like me – I heard you say it yourself."

"When?" she demanded, having no recollection of ever saying she didn't want him.

"At Whitehall's wedding. You said you wanted a man of strength, and breadth, who enjoyed excitement and could show you adventure. I am the complete opposite of such a man."

She took a breath. She had said that. In fact, it was one of the very reasons she had initially opposed her attraction to Noah.

"That was before I knew you."

"You mean, before you changed me."

There was an edge to his voice, and she eyed him. "What has overcome you?"

He ignored her question.

"You changed me into the man you wanted. Altered my appearance, told me how you wanted me to speak, to flirt. It was only then that you had any interest in me."

Percy rubbed her forehead in frustration. Goodness, this man could be ornery, analyzing every word, every moment.

Why could he not understand that none of it mattered if what they felt for one another was true?

"It was what caused me to take greater awareness of you, yes, but I would never want to be with you simply for how you look or how you flirt. It is you that I want, Noah. One of the reasons I want you is because you understand that I need to make my own decisions and you do not try to keep me back from what I choose to do. So do not start telling me my own mind now."

He ran a hand through his hair. "Then why did you not outright deny Lord Stephen?"

"He *is* everything I *thought* I wanted. As it turns out, I did not quite know my own mind. When I am with him, I do not wish for him to touch me or to hold me as I wish for you to do."

"It is only because of what we did together. Although I would suggest you find another. Lord Stephen does not seem to hold much respect for your wishes."

"You are telling me what I think again," she said, placing her hands on her hips. "And I do not like it."

"Percy, I am leaving Bath in the next few days," he said quietly, and she wished that he would show some emotion, would shout or growl or do anything but just stand there and speak facts to her. "I wanted to tell you and to wish you farewell."

"So this is goodbye." She heard the crack in her voice and willed away the pain that was rising through her stomach, doing all she could to turn it into anger.

"Yes."

"You are not going to fight for me?"

"I am doing this *for* you."

She stepped toward him, raising her finger and pointing it into his chest. "Do you know something? You are no better than the woman who left you."

"Percy—"

"No," she said, blinking furiously to prevent the tears from falling. "You are a fool. A fool who is giving up on what could be a lifetime of happiness together."

She walked over to the door, opening it and gesturing out. "Leave."

"Percy, I do not want it to be like this."

"I said get out!" she said, but then was completely unprepared when he walked over, stopped in front of her, and leaned down and kissed her, hard.

She wished she had it within her to push him away, to slap him and tell him to leave her be, but instead, she kissed him back as the tears began to fall from her eyes. Finally, she had the wherewithal to do what she should have from the start, as she pushed him back and the sobs threatened.

"I need you to go."

"I'm sorry, I—"

"Go!" she choked out between sobs as she pulled the ring off her finger and threw it at him. He caught it just before she pushed him out the door, shutting it behind him as firmly as she could, before sinking against it, placing her head in her hands, and allowing all of the emotion she hadn't known she possessed to break free.

It was where Cassandra found her minutes later, and she allowed her friend to take her in her arms and provide her with all of the comforts that she needed.

It was then that she made a vow. She would never give another man her heart. For it hurt far too much.

CHAPTER 25

"Explain this to me again," Eric said as they rode beside the carriage toward Castleton. "You are in love with a woman who appears to return that love, she is everything you always wanted and more, she practically begged you to marry her, and you told her no, that she should marry someone else."

Noah shot him an annoyed look. "It is more complicated than that."

"But am I correct?"

"I suppose."

Eric shook his head in dismay. "You are an idiot."

"Percy said the same."

"She was right. What's wrong with you, man?"

"This is best for the long term. She wouldn't be happy with me in the years to come."

"Says who? You?"

"Women tire of me."

Eric snorted. "Letitia tired of you, but she was not right for you. She was waiting for someone else to come along.

That's the difference. Lady Percy wants you for the man you are."

Noah sighed. "Can we not speak of this anymore?"

"Fine," Eric said, waving a hand in the air. "I am glad that I have at least convinced you to accompany me to Castleton. How long will you stay?"

"I will leave as soon as you let me," Noah said with a humorless laugh. "I'd like to return to London and take advantage of some of the offers I have received."

"You know you can set whatever schedule you would like."

"I am aware," Noah said. "I will likely also spend some time in the country at the home that you have so graciously provided me."

"We have two country homes, Noah, and it is not as though I have done anything besides being born first to deserve both of them. Besides, it is far too much for one man to take care of. You might as well help. In fact, you will be doing me a favor."

Noah nodded. He was telling Eric what he wanted to hear, but in truth, he couldn't imagine how lonely he would be in a large country home without anyone to share it with, his mind free to picture Percy in her new life with her new husband. At least in London, he could keep his mind preoccupied.

"Tell me something, Eric," he said, his lips curling. His brother had taken a great deal of interest in his personal life. Perhaps it was time for him to question Eric himself. "Are you ever going to tell Lady Faith how you feel?"

Eric turned to look at him so abruptly that he nearly fell off his horse, and Noah snickered with the first bit of mirth he had felt since he had left Percy.

"Why would you think that I feel anything for her?"

"I have heard you mention your interest before."

Eric shrugged in an obvious attempt at nonchalance, but he was not a man who easily hid his emotion.

"I find her attractive."

"And?"

"And that's it," Eric said defensively. "There is nothing more to discuss."

"Very well," Noah said. "Then no more discussions about *any* women, understood?"

Eric sighed dramatically and rolled his eyes. "It is not the same. Not at all." He caught Noah's expression. "Very well. No more discussions. But do promise me you will not mope around Castleton over the next week?"

"I do not mope."

"Noah."

"Very well," he said. "No moping."

* * *

Percy sat miserably at the dining room table, unable to conjure even a false smile. She was completely at odds with the rest of her dinner companions, composed of her family and Lord Stephen's.

Even the return of her brother could not bring mirth to her countenance. She could sense his frown at her from down the table, for he knew her well, and was aware when she was bothered.

Lady Jane and her parents had accompanied them, for which Percy was happy, as she knew what it likely meant – and, from what she could tell, Lady Jane seemed amiable enough. Percy just hadn't managed enough interest to make her acquaintance. The woman likely thought her horrible, but she couldn't help it. Not at the moment.

She stared at Lord Stephen across the table, a large smile on his handsome face as he charmed her mother. She tried desperately to picture a life with him, but the only man she could see beside her was Noah. Noah as he looked since she had helped him change his appearance and countenance, or Noah from before. She honestly didn't care – if only he could see the truth in that.

She was grateful that her father had not yet asked her for a decision as to marriage to Lord Stephen, for she had no idea what she would say. The truth as to why she had not yet answered was because she had reasoned if she couldn't have Noah, did it matter who she spent her life with?

Lord Stephen must have sensed her perusal, for he turned and met her eye. She tried to smile at him, to show him some attention – but then he smugly smirked, as though believing her to be enamored with him, and her stomach roiled as a wave of nausea washed over her.

She couldn't do it.

Not just because she wanted Noah – although she wondered if that would ever change – but because she had to be true to herself. She wouldn't spend her life with a man just because she had no other option.

She would rather be alone – no matter the consequences.

"Percy, you are so quiet," Rebecca said from across the table, and Percy shrugged a shoulder.

"I am tired."

"From what? Were you out late last night?"

"No," she said slowly. "I have had much on my mind."

"Oh, I completely understand," Elizabeth said from her seat next to Percy. "There is so much to consider, especially when one is not from Bath. Where is best to visit each evening? With whom should we socialize? Which young men —" She stopped when she realized that Lord Stephen was listening, a red flush creeping up her cheeks.

"Do go on," Lord Stephen said, resting his chin on his fist. "I am enjoying listening to you speak. Your voice is melodic."

Melodic? Percy could use many words to describe Elizabeth's voice, and melodic was most certainly not one of them. A grin began to spread over her face at what that could mean. Was Lord Stephen interested in her cousin? Oh, but that would be wonderful. For then it could mean that Lord Stephen would pursue Elizabeth and she would be free to--

Her head snapped around in horror as her father's chair scraped against the floor when he pushed it backward, for she knew exactly what that meant. He held his glass in one hand and his spoon in the other, dinging it against the glass to gather their attention.

"Thank you all for joining us this evening," he said, lifting his glass to all of them. "I am so grateful to have my family together – and I do consider all of you family."

Please just announce Richard's engagement.

"First, my son, Richard, has been ever so dutiful. Not only is he learning from me on the responsibilities that will be his one day, but he has chosen a woman to accompany him in his life who is everything we would ever want in a daughter."

Percy frowned but said nothing.

"Of course, that does not mean we do not equally appreciate our daughter, Persephone," he said, turning his attention to her, and Percy swallowed hard. She tried to smile but her lips would not obey. "She is also—"

No, no, no. If she let this happen, there would be no turning back.

Before he could continue, Percy pushed her chair away from the table so quickly that it would have fallen over had a quick-acting footman not reached out and caught it. She had to stop this, and while she knew she was making a scene, it would be far better than reneging on an announced betrothal.

"Excuse me," she said, and ran from the room, barely registering the shocked expressions that followed her.

THE SCHOLAR'S KEY

She stopped in the corridor outside of the dining room, her back pressed against the wall, her breath coming fast as a sheen of perspiration covered her brow. She placed her hand on her stomach, willing the anxious nausea away.

With her eyes closed and her focus on calming herself, she didn't notice her mother's presence until her hands were on top of hers, holding them steady. Percy finally blinked her eyes open, finding her mother's concerned face right in front of hers.

"Percy," her mother said softly, "what is the matter?"

"I can't do it," Percy said in an urgent whisper. "I cannot marry him. Father was about to announce it, wasn't he?"

Her mother looked one way and then the next before taking her hand and leading her toward another room, pushing open the door to the softly lit parlor and closing it behind them. She sat down on the sofa and patted the space next to her. Percy sank down, her satiny soft pale blue skirts billowing around her as she did.

"Yes, your father was about to announce the engagement. When you didn't provide him with an answer, he decided for you."

Percy shook her head desperately back and forth, tears welling in her eyes – tears of frustration that everyone, even Noah, seemed to be making decisions for her, as well as tears of grief that the life she had wished for had been so close yet remained out of reach.

"I cannot marry Lord Stephen," she said, determination mixing with her despair. "I have tried, Mother, but I feel nothing for him. The thought of his touch only causes me repulsion, not affection."

Once again, her mother laid her hands over Percy's, her expression sympathetic. "Perhaps that will grow over time."

"It will not," Percy said, leaning in toward her. "For I know what it is like to desire the touch of a man, and with

Lord Stephen, I feel the opposite. The truth is, Mother, I would rather be alone than be with a man that I do not love."

"I wish that you could do as you please, Percy, but a woman cannot live alone."

"Why not? Many women do."

"And the only ones who live comfortably are widows and prostitutes."

"I will find my way," Percy said stubbornly. "I am sure I will. One day, when Father can no longer support me, I know that Richard will. My brother may be a pain, but he loves me, and I will promise him that I will stay out of Lady Jane's way."

"Oh, Percy," her mother said with sorrow. "This is not the life I wish for you. What of Mr. Rowley?"

Percy's head shot up at his name. "What about him?"

"He is the man whose touch you crave, is it not?"

Percy's cheeks burned. "Yes, but he does not want me."

"I can hardly believe that to be true."

"He says that it is better this way. I tried to convince him otherwise, but he would not accept. If that is what he feels, then so be it. He has made his choice. Now I must make mine."

"Very well," her mother said, defeat on her face. "I will talk to your father. Now, go up to your bedchamber and I will make your excuses. I will say that you have become ill."

"Thank you, Mother," Percy said, leaning in and wrapping her arms around her in an embrace. "Thank you ever so much."

Grateful that she had at least one person in her life she could count on, Percy did as her mother said and returned to her bedroom, where she began to pack. Cassandra had asked her to accompany her to Castleton, and Percy realized it was likely the only scenario in which her father would provide respite in attempting to find her a husband.

She knew her parents would not be pleased with this decision either, but she had to leave Bath. It held far too many memories.

Memories she needed to leave behind – just as Noah had chosen to do to her.

CHAPTER 26

"After this, I am finished with traveling for a long time," Noah said to Eric as they arrived at Castleton. "I feel as though I have been all over England and back in the past year, what with weddings and house parties and my stay in Bath."

"I rather enjoy it myself," Eric said with a grin. "I like to be on the move. I find myself becoming rather stagnant when staying in one place."

"And yet you have so much to look after."

"I believe I do a fine job of it," Eric said defensively. "Besides, you know Mother is the one truly in charge."

Noah smirked at that, for it was the truth. Not that Eric minded – he far preferred to do as he wished and not worry about any burdens. Which was why he was currently planning to travel to Spain.

Castleton, despite requiring some upkeep, was as welcoming as ever, but Noah couldn't help the nostalgic emptiness that filled him when he walked through the door. It was caused, of course, by the fact that, on this visit to the estate, Percy wouldn't be here. Even before, when she had barely looked at him, at least she had been in his presence.

Now, he had ensured that would never happen again.

They had arrived with Ashford and had all agreed to meet for a drink in the billiards room before dinner. Ashford's sister and Covington were not arriving for another few days, which meant that it was only Ashford's parents who were also in the country home, and they had declined the dinner invitation, as they typically did when the duke was not in his right mind.

"Are your rooms comfortable?" Ashford asked when he walked in, a paper folded in his hand.

"Yes, as always," Eric said before Ashford sat on the large leather chesterfield, crossing one leg over the other.

"Good," Ashford said. "Hopefully, someday shortly, we will be able to update them. Someday when my coffers are filled again."

A longing filled his eyes, and Noah and Eric exchanged a look as Noah shifted uncomfortably in his chair. He knew how much Ashford was counting on all of them now to help find this treasure, and he didn't want to let his friend down – even if there might be nothing they could do to ensure that it would be found.

"Anyway, it appears some news has reached us."

"Oh?"

"My mother received word from one of her friends in Bath that she was going to attend an engagement party. It must have been held by now."

Noah, not one to ever be much interested in gossip, was not particularly listening to this turn of conversation – until he heard just who was hosting the party.

"The party was at the Assembly Rooms and was to be hosted by Lord Fairfax."

"Lord Fairfax – Lady Percy's father?" Eric murmured, his

gaze upon Noah. "How interesting. Was it Lady Percy's engagement?"

"She didn't say, but I would assume so. I had heard a betrothal with Lord Stephen was forthcoming." He paused. "I am not sure what to make of that. I know the man, and I cannot see him being a good husband to Lady Percy. We shall have to see what Cassandra has to say about it once she arrives. She will certainly not contain her opinion, and I know she spent time with Lady Percy in Bath. I am sure she would have attended the party."

All the blood seemed to be draining from Noah's head as he sat there, ringing filling his ears and panic bubbling through his chest. He had known that it was likely Percy would become betrothed to Lord Stephen, but now that he knew the truth of it, it was more than he could bear.

"Rowley? Are you all right?"

Ashford was speaking, but his voice seemed far away as Noah stood, stumbling backward a step.

"Fine," he said. "Just need some air."

He rushed from the room as quickly as he was able, down the corridor and out the closest door, taking deep breaths.

Percy was right. He was a fool. He could have had her as his wife. He could have made her happy. Sure, maybe he wasn't exactly what she had thought she wanted, but he would never have hurt her, would always have been faithful, and would have shown her every day just how wonderful she was.

He had thought she would find another man — a better man. But Lord Stephen would do none of those things. He would marry her, then leave her to wonder if she was good enough, while he spent time with other women, not realizing just how lucky he was to have a woman like her.

Noah never should have said farewell.

Now he no longer had the decision to make. It was a decision that he realized he should have made *with* Percy – not *for* her.

And there was nothing he could do about it anymore.

* * *

"I AM SO pleased that you chose to accompany us," Cassandra said as the carriage turned up the drive toward Castleton. Through the carriage window, the estate rose behind Lord Covington, Cassandra's husband, who was riding beside them.

"Thank you for inviting me," Percy said. "I needed to leave Bath. Thank goodness my mother allowed me to accompany you, now that you are a married woman and, therefore, a proper companion. She would have escorted us, but she said she needed to clean up the mess I left behind."

Cassandra patted Percy's knee when she pulled a face. "At least she is allowing you to do as you please. How did your father accept your decision?"

"Not well," Percy said, shaking her head as she remembered her father's blustering. He had tried every threat, but in the end, Percy hadn't cared about any of them. She would not be marrying Lord Stephen, and it was best to stop it now before it went too far. Her father had intoned on and on about the family's humiliation, but what was Percy to do?

"Thankfully, Richard and Mother intervened and calmed Father down. Richard promised that I would always have a home with him. Lady Jane agreed although I sensed she wasn't quite as pleased about it."

"You know that any of us would also welcome you. Even now, Gideon is pleased to have you at Castleton. I wonder when he arrived," Cassandra mused. "He left a few days before us, saying he had much to attend to. He is still desperately trying to turn our family fortunes around and is helping Lord Ferrington prepare for his journey to Spain."

Percy absently nodded. Cassandra's father had become ill and spent all of their fortunes, and now Lord Ashford had to do his utmost to try to pay back their debts. He had placed a great deal of hope in this treasure hunt that she wasn't sure would amount to anything.

"It is nearing the dinner hour," Cassandra said as they walked into the house, the butler, Clarkson, greeting them. Percy caught his eye as she passed, and she wondered at the scrutiny he was giving her. He likely hadn't been prepared for her presence. "Why do you not settle in and then we will meet in the drawing room?"

"Wonderful," Percy said, but her heart was heavy as she climbed the grand staircase. The last time she had been here, so had Noah – although she had only then seen him as an acquaintance. Still, she hadn't been prepared for how the association would assault her.

She could almost swear she could smell him too, the hint of cinnamon which clung to him. His presence was within these walls, taunting her. She should have just returned home to their country estate, but there was no one there but the servants.

With the help of her lady's maid, who had accompanied them, she changed for the evening into her favorite cream silk, which she hoped would make her feel up to being pleasant company.

As she sat and ran her hands over the dress, all she could think about was Noah removing it from her body. Mary had pinned her hair up and all that Percy could picture was Noah removing the pins and letting it fall, lacing his fingers in her strands.

Familiar tears of frustration welled in her eyes. Was this

to be the rest of her life, then, him following her wherever she went?

Now was not the time to consider it, however, for Cassandra and her family would be waiting. Percy lifted her skirts as she stood and walked out the door, eager to finish this dinner and crawl into bed, where she hoped, tonight, her dreams would give her a respite and not contain the man who had rejected her. It was time to banish him from her thoughts, in turn. It was the one place where she should, at least, have total control.

Percy descended the stairs and was just about to turn into the drawing room when Cassandra came hurrying around the corner, her relief evident when she saw Percy.

"Oh, thank goodness, there you are," she said. "I need to tell you something—"

Percy wasn't able to hear anything else she said, however. For at that moment, her head turned, her body reacting before she even realized who had so surprised her.

Noah.

She stopped, blinked, and froze in place as they locked eyes. He was just walking out of the drawing room as she was stepping in. His shoulders were slouched, his gait was slow, and she was sure that it was pain she saw in the depths of those hazel eyes that she knew so well.

Percy took one step back, and then another, shock, anguish, and desire all welling up in her, each fighting with the other for dominance.

Finally, she couldn't take it anymore.

She turned and ran.

* * *

No one had told him she would be here.

Noah had spent the last two days doing exactly what he

had promised Eric he wouldn't do – mope. How could he not after learning that the woman he would love for the rest of his life was going to marry another man?

Especially when the reason she was doing so was all because of him and his stupidity.

It had been bad enough before, but how was he supposed to handle it now that he had to be in her presence? She obviously had no wish to speak to him. She had made that clear the last time they had seen one another, and now, when she ran away at the simple sight of him.

"What did you do to her?" Ashford asked, looking back and forth between him and Percy's retreating form as he stepped out of the room to see what was wrong. Lady Covington was biting her lip as she watched Noah, as though she had something she wanted to say but was afraid to say it.

"He turned her away," Lady Covington finally burst out, apparently no longer able to contain her words.

"What?" Ashford said, looking from his sister to Noah and back again, his confusion evident. "Right now?"

"No, in Bath. He refused her affections."

Ashford scratched his head. "I thought she was marrying Lord Stephen."

"No," Lady Covington said, shaking her head dramatically. "Her father wanted her to, but she told him that she couldn't."

At those words, hope began to glow in Noah's body, starting in his stomach and rising through his chest.

"She didn't agree to it?" he said.

"But what of the engagement party?" Ashford asked, his brow furrowed.

"That was for her brother," Lady Covington said with obvious exasperation at their inability to keep up with the conversation. "He is marrying Lady Jane Montgomery."

Noah began to walk backwards away from them.

"Rowley, where are you going?" Ashford asked.

"There is something I have to do," he said. "And I have to do it now."

And with that, he turned and sprinted away, out the doors that Percy had exited.

He did know what he had to do – he just had no idea how he was going to do it.

CHAPTER 27

Noah ran out to the gardens through the terrace doors, his head swiveling one way and the next as he searched for Percy. Finally, he saw the glint of her hair when the sun kissed it, across the gardens as she was still moving, toward the lake on the other side.

He took off at a run as fast as he could, not stopping to consider what he was going to say when he caught her. All he knew was that he needed to get to her now.

"Percy!" he called out, but she was too far away to hear him. He rounded the rather unkempt gardens now, seeing that she was making for the lake in the distance. He wondered if she had any idea where she was going or why, but wherever her direction, he would follow.

She finally stopped, her shoulders rising and falling so dramatically that he knew she was either out of breath or upset, standing at the edge of the lake, her arms crossed around herself as she stared out at the water.

Noah was so focused on her that he missed the tree root in front of him, and when his toe hit the edge, he went flying down the bank of the lake, his shoulder hitting the ground as he rolled right into the shallow water.

"Noah!"

He spit water and seaweed out of his mouth as he looked up at Percy, who was staring at him from the bank with her mouth open in shock.

"Are you all right?"

"Yes," he muttered as he got to his feet, shaking his head like a dog, Percy taking a step backward to prevent getting soaked.

"What are you doing?" she asked, her hands dropping into fists at her side. "Why are you here? Why are you chasing me? Why will you not just leave me alone?"

Noah sighed as he pushed his wet hair back away from his forehead, sliding off his spectacles to attempt to dry them. He removed his jacket and set it on the ground, searching for dry linen beneath, and finally, Percy took pity on him.

"Here," she said impatiently, holding her hand out, and he passed her the glasses, which she surprisingly gently rubbed dry on her skirts and then passed back to him.

He set them on his nose, before holding out his hand to her. "Will you sit with me?"

"No," she said stubbornly, and he couldn't fault her for it.

"I made a mistake," he said, lifting his arms to the side, deciding it was best to be honest. "Make that two mistakes."

He saw the glimmer in her eye as she was, apparently, at least interested in what he had to say.

"I pushed you away," he said. "That was the first. The second was not listening to you."

"I'd say *that* was your first mistake," she said, crossing her arms again.

"Very well. That was the first," he said, stepping toward her, taking a deep breath, speaking in halting tones. "I have learned my lesson, Percy. I thought that I was preventing both of us from a future where we would be unhappy, but I was wrong. I heard of an engagement in your family and when I assumed it was that of you and Lord Stephen, I realized that accepting a man who you wouldn't have chosen for yourself was what would lead to a lifetime in which neither of us was happy. And I had pushed you to it. It was stupid. I was stupid. I was protecting myself from being hurt again. I was worried that you didn't want me for who I truly was, but even if I have to be the man you want me to be and not myself, then it would be better than being without you."

Her face fell at that, as she listened to him earnestly, and she walked over and took his hands in hers.

"You are still wrong."

That wasn't what he was expecting.

"I am?"

"Yes," she said, her lips slightly curling upward. "It is not that I do not want you for the man you are. Yes, we changed your look and practiced flirtation, but I told you, that only caused me to notice you. It didn't change who you truly are, and you can look however you want, I do not care. I just want you. The man who has shown me what it means to be cherished, and treasured, who has allowed me to be myself and has welcomed my faults and allowed me to choose my own path. And if you will accept it, then I choose *you*, Noah Rowley. I said no to Lord Stephen. If I cannot have the man that I love, then I will have no man at all."

Noah wished he wasn't covered in lake water so that he could properly take her in his arms, but she didn't seem to care.

"Percy," he said, holding her hands in his, which would have to do for now. "I love you. I think I have always loved you. I want to provide you with the life that you deserve, and while yes, I will likely spend a great deal of time with my head down in books, the rest of it will be spent treasuring you."

"I love you too," she said, linking her arms around his neck. "I am happy how ever we live our lives, as long as it is together."

"I do not deserve you," he murmured, and she laughed.

"Wrong again," she said. "We deserve each other. Now, Noah, you must be catching a chill." There was a gleam in her eyes now. "Why do we not properly dry your clothes before we return?"

He looked around them, and while there was no one about, he was still uncertain. "You do know that even us being alone likely means you will be ruined?"

"Oh dear," she said with a fake pout. "Does that mean we will have to be married?"

He chuckled. "Likely."

"Well," she said with a dramatic sigh, "so be it."

She began to work the buttons free on his waistcoat before sliding it off of his arms. She picked up his jacket as well and laid both out on a nearby rock.

"I think we can leave my shirt on," he murmured, but she pursed her lips and shook her head.

"I think not," she said, undoing the button and then lifting the shirt over his head before running her hands over his chest and abdomen.

"Percy?"

"Yes?"

"Will you marry me, in truth?"

"Of course I will," she said, leaning in and kissing him soundly. "It is about time you asked."

She unfastened his breeches, freeing him, and he was immediately hard and ready for her.

"What do we have here?" she said teasingly. "Is this for me?"

"Always," he said. "It is yours now."

She led him over to the side of the path, where there was a slight clearing in the trees. He looked around, unsure if this was the right decision, and she laughed at his hesitation.

"It's fine," she said, "I promise. What's the worst that can happen?"

"Well—"

She silenced him then by pulling him in toward her, fusing her lips over his. All of his uncertainty faded in a flash, as he was completely overcome by Percy. Cherry blossoms scented the air around her while a hint of strawberry tickled his tongue. She was soft in his arms, pliant yet equally as exuberant.

She was his, she was home, she was heaven.

How he ever thought he could have lived without her was a mystery, for Noah realized at that moment that he would give up everything for her – but fortunately, she would never ask it of him.

And he loved her for it.

They fell onto the ground together, her skirts softening the fall.

His heart began pounding so hard against his ribs that he wondered whether Percy could hear it, but when she kissed him again, his breath came easier, as she was more vital to him than air itself. He kissed her slowly, gently at first, until a great need sparked within him and the slowly burning embers between them burst into flame.

He needed her – all of her. And now that he knew he had her heart, it seemed that anything else was possible.

He opened his mouth to tell her so, but then realized that, in this moment, no words were necessary. They could simply be in this moment together. Tendrils of her hair had fallen out and were now splayed around her head in the grass, and she lifted her hands and weaved them into his own hair and pulled him down toward her. She wrapped her legs around him, and he slowly lifted her skirts until they fanned out as he lay between her bent knees, finding her bare, waiting for him.

There was no time for him to remove her dress, no time for them to play with one another. Noah could barely contain his need for Percy, and he placed one more quick kiss upon her lips to ensure she understood his need for her, and her alone, before he sheathed himself inside her.

She moaned, and he stopped, worried that he had hurt her, but then she spread her legs wider and he buried his head in her neck as he wrapped his hands around her hips and pulled out of her before thrusting in once more. He filled her, seated fully within, before rocking back, in and out in a rhythm that was as natural as breathing itself.

Noah had never imagined the depth of passionate emotion that was possible. Percy had sparked a light within him that, he now realized, hadn't changed him, but rather had awakened another side of him that he hadn't known existed.

Her legs gripped him tighter around his waist, urging him on, closer, faster, as her arms wrapped around his neck, and he knew that she would always challenge him, always help him to be the very best of himself.

He lost all sense of time as he was overwhelmed by her surrounding him, the wind rustling in the trees above them, the water lapping against the shore, their breath hard and intermingling.

Percy surprised him when she rocked upward against him, then pushed him backward until he was the one lying on the ground.

"What—"

She didn't let him speak, however, as she grinned wickedly before she lifted her skirts and straddled him, sinking over top of him as her head dropped backward. She rode him slowly at first, becoming used to the rhythm, before she increased her speed, and he lifted his hands, freeing her breasts from her bodice. She squeezed him when he tweaked her nipples, and then as she began to rock harder, faster, she tightened around him, her hands dropping to rake her nails over his shoulders as her breath quickened.

Her response was all that was required to send Noah over the edge, and he bit down on his lip to keep from crying out as he found his release inside her.

She collapsed against him, and he ran his hand over her hair as he held her with the other. He closed his eyes, listening to the wind through the trees, the water on the shore, the birds above, and Percy's breath against him.

She shifted so that she was lying beside him, her head on his stomach, her palm splayed over his chest. His heart constricted, as he could hardly believe that she was real, and she had chosen him to bestow her love upon.

"Eric is leaving," he said softly, kissing her hair.

"I know," she said softly. "He shall have a grand adventure."

He had worried from the start that she would prefer a man like Eric, who could offer her such moments in life, but her tone didn't seem to hold any wistfulness.

"You don't mind being with a man who would prefer to stay at his estate, or in the libraries of universities?"

She shook her head. "Not if that man is you."

"I think I finally believe you," he said in wonderment, and she laughed softly as she snuggled in closer toward him, wiggling her hips against his as her fingers drew circles over his chest. "I apologize for not listening for so long."

"Some lessons must be learned the hard way, I suppose," she said, chuckling and he kissed the top of her head.

"We should probably return," he said. "They are going to wonder where we are."

"Oh, I think they have a pretty good idea," Percy said, propping her chin on top of her hands on his chest. "At least, Cassandra does, I'm sure."

"What kind of books do you ladies read, anyway?" he asked incredulously, to which she laughed. Covington had casually mentioned the women's reading club before, but Noah hadn't believed that their choice of books had truly been so scandalous. Now, he had a much better idea. And Covington was right. They had served them well.

"I have something for you," he said, reaching for his clothes and picking through them until he found the right pocket. A wide smile broke out on Percy's face.

"My ring."

"Your ring," he said, holding her hand in his, sliding it onto her finger with the other. "This time, I hope you wear it as my promise. My promise to make you mine."

"Always," she whispered.

"I will give you the best life I can," he said, planting a kiss on the top of her head.

"I know you will," she said with a smile. "Just by being you."

CHAPTER 28

"We have a letter from Aunt Eve," Lord Ashford said a few nights later, as their party had assembled in the drawing room after dinner.

Their numbers had grown, as Faith had made the short journey from the nearby Newfield Hall. When she had announced her intentions to attend, her sister, Hope, and her new husband, Lord Whitehall, had also been encouraged to meet them here. The only one they were missing now from their group was Madeline, but it would have taken her too long to travel to meet with the rest of them.

"Mrs. Compton is a most interesting woman, is she not, Noah?" Percy said, leaning forward and placing her hand on Noah's thigh. They had made no secret of their feelings for one another and had told the rest of their party that they would soon be married. Percy had written her parents and was waiting for their response. She assumed from her previous conversation with her mother that her engagement would be welcomed, although she was slightly unsure of her father. Noah had sent his own note, in the hopes of determining when they would be in the same area so that he might ask for Percy's hand.

"She is," he agreed. "You have a most interesting family history, Ashford."

"So we do," Cassandra said. "And it is time we told Aunt Eve about its most recent history. She deserves to know, and the next time we see her, we will be sure to share. It is such a pity that the jewels were lost again. I know they are worth something, but it is more than that. They have such significance for our family. My grandfather gifted them to my grandmother many years ago."

"I was worried they might be stolen again," Noah said. "It seemed so easy for the thief to capture them the first time. Why would he – or she – not do so again?"

They began to debate who might have stolen the jewels when the butler appeared in the doorway, clearing his throat. "Excuse me, my lord," he said, with a bow toward Lord Ashford, "but a package has arrived for you."

"From the post?" Ashford said, walking over and accepting it.

"No," the butler said. "It was on the doorstep in a box."

"I see," Ashford said with interest. He placed the package down on the table in the middle of the room before carefully opening the lid. "Well, I'll be."

He reached in and pulled out the ruby necklace, much to the shock of everyone in the room.

"I don't understand," he murmured. "Why would this be stolen only to be returned? We are in the country. It is not as though we are in London with a great deal of passersby each day."

"And the necklace went missing in Bath, which is a fair distance away," Noah said, walking over and holding out his hand. "May I see it?"

"Of course," Ashford said, passing it over, and Noah

immediately nodded as he checked the back of the heart, where the keyhole was.

"This is the same necklace," he said.

Ashford was tapping his chin with his index finger.

"Do you still have the key?"

"I do," Noah said, fishing it out of his pocket, where he had kept it close.

"Try turning it again — just to ensure that nothing else is within."

"Very well," Noah said, taking no offence at Ashford's request. They had, after all, been fairly excited about their discovery last time.

He pulled the key out, placed it in the hole, and turned it — to find the empty space inside.

"There is not much room," he said, passing the necklace to Ashford — but as Ashford put his hand to one side and Noah was just releasing the other, there was a clinking sound, and a piece broke off in Noah's hand.

"Bollocks," Noah whispered under his breath, looking up at Ashford's astonished face. "My apologies, I—"

"Wait a moment," Ashford said. "I do not think that it's broken."

He held his hand out for the piece, which Noah passed over.

"You see?" He said. "It can snap right back in, but also — it is the perfect size to hold in your hand. Perhaps this is part of the next clue."

"But what could it be?" Percy asked, and Noah looked around to find they had all moved in close.

"I have no idea," Ashford said, shaking his head. "I suppose that will be up to Ferrington to find out."

"So whoever stole the necklace just... gave it back?" Lord Whitehall said incredulously from his chair in the shadows of the room, the one of them who had not joined their circle.

"Apparently," Ashford said.

"Are you sure about this next step?" Hope asked with hesitation. "From the name of one city in Spain, Lord Ferrington is going to travel across the ocean to look for... what? How will he even know where to go, what to do?"

"I'm sure I'll figure it out," Lord Ferrington said cheerfully. "I'm a rather resourceful sort. Besides, my Spanish is exemplary, and I am a friendly sort, so I will get along well with the local people."

Faith snorted, although her sister reprimanded her with just a look. Faith was as cynical as Hope was optimistic.

Percy couldn't help but look at Lord Ferrington with some pity. Noah had told her that his brother had always been a bit in love with Faith, although Percy could hardly understand his infatuation. Faith was one of her closest friends, and she loved her like a sister, but she had always treated Lord Ferrington with derision, as she had apparently thought he was rather a pompous sort. It was quite interesting how different he and Noah were from one another. Perhaps Lord Ferrington's heart wanted what it couldn't have.

It wasn't until the next morning when she and Faith were walking together down the small river that led away from the lake that she was able to better understand Faith's opinion on Lord Ferrington and his intentions.

"What do you think of Lord Ferrington's plan to travel to Spain?" Percy asked as she trailed her fingers along the lush greenery that bordered the river. It was not well manicured here like the estate gardens, but rather wild and free, the greenery painting its majesty on the canvas it had been provided.

"I think that he is using this for an adventure himself," she said.

"Are not all the men of his acquaintance interested in

daring pursuits? It is, after all, what initially drew them together," Percy said, not worried about Faith's response. The two of them had always been this way – sharing their complete truths, secure in the knowledge that any response would be made and met in truth and love.

"Yes, but why suddenly volunteer to visit the Continent?" Faith persisted. "The man is an earl. He has responsibilities. Who is going to look after them while he's sailing away on some silly pursuit to find a treasure?"

"I suppose that is for him to be concerned about," Percy said lightly, attempting to hide her smile at how concerned Faith was over the man's affairs.

"I do not trust him."

"Whyever not?" Percy asked, surprised. She knew Faith wasn't keen on Lord Ferrington but couldn't understand why she would say such a thing. She had thought them all to be acquaintances on friendly terms.

"Due to an experience," she said hastily. "It is nothing to note."

"Faith," Percy said, peering at her, "are you keeping something from me?"

Faith sighed, staring out over the water before turning to Percy, her blue eyes insistent. "I will tell you, but you must promise me that you will never tell anyone else. Not even Hope knows."

"Of course," Percy said.

"Especially Noah."

Percy bit her lip. That was a much harder promise to make. She didn't like the thought of keeping secrets from Noah, especially when they concerned his brother.

"I'm not sure..."

"Percy, please?"

Faith never asked anyone for anything. She was always the one who took it upon herself to be there for others, to take care of them, to make sure that all was well. The fact that she was asking Percy, and with such supplication in her eyes, meant that she truly needed to speak to someone about this.

"Very well."

"I know that Lord Ferrington is interested in me because he told me."

"Did he?" Percy said, stopping where they walked, her eyes wide. "What did you say?"

"Nothing. I didn't have a chance before he kissed me."

"Oh, Faith!" Percy exclaimed, bringing her hands up to her face. "How wonderful."

"Yes, it was actually," Faith said, a blush stealing up her cheeks, but her mouth remained in a grim line. "Until I saw him kiss another that same night."

"He didn't," Percy said incredulously.

"He did," Faith said, nodding her head. "It was at one of my mother's parties a few years ago. He whispered me those sweet nothings in the garden, kissed me, and then when I went to find him later, he was in an alcove near the ballroom, with another woman on his lips."

"Oh, Faith," Percy said, seeing the pain in her eyes. Here she had thought that Faith didn't like Eric, as she supposed she could call him now that he was going to be her brother-in-law, when all along it was the opposite. Faith had been hurt. "What did he say when you asked him about it?"

"Nothing, because I never mentioned it."

"You didn't?"

"No," Faith said, shaking her head. "It hurt my pride far too much. I did not want him to know how much he had hurt me. I didn't want anyone to know. It was far easier to pretend that it had never happened."

"I see," Percy said softly. "It must be hard, having to see him time and again when we all gather."

"Yes, it is," Faith said. "It is hard. I want nothing to do with him, and yet I also look forward to seeing him every time. I believe I am as angry with myself as I am with him. How terrible is that?"

"Not terrible at all," Percy said, shaking her head. "Human emotion is a fickle thing."

"And now, after everything that we have all done – Cassandra and Lord Covington, my sister and Lord Whitehall, you and Mr. Rowley – we are going to trust *him*, the greatest rogue among us, with solving the next clue? This means so much to Lord Ashford and his family. What if he makes a mess of this?"

Percy shrugged. "If Lord Ashford is putting his faith in him, I suppose we must as well."

"I don't like it," Faith said, shaking her head. "I don't like it at all."

"Well," Percy said with a shrug, "there is nothing we can do about it."

"Perhaps," Faith murmured with a gleam in her eye that worried Percy. "Perhaps not."

* * *

It was with some sadness that they all said their farewells a few nights later. Noah was particularly going to miss his brother, and he could tell Percy was forcing her smile for her friends.

"What's wrong?" he asked, turning and cupping her face in his hands when they headed back inside.

"It's just that we all used to see one another so often, and now it is so uncertain when we will see one another again. It used to be that we always knew we would all be back in London when the season began, but now with Cassandra expecting a baby and Hope leaving to travel with her husband, it could be some time until we all come together once more."

"I promise you that we will always make every effort to see them, whenever you wish," Noah said, wiping a tear away from her cheek.

"Thank you," Percy said with a grateful smile.

Besides Lord Ashford and Lord and Lady Covington, they would be the last to leave. They had finally heard back from Percy's family, and her parents offered to come to them before beginning preparations for their wedding. As expected, Percy's mother seemed quite overjoyed by their betrothal, if one could read into her words on paper. Noah still suspected Percy's father would not be quite as pleased as he would have been with Lord Stephen, but it seemed his daughter's happiness did count for something.

"I am still intrigued as to how this is all going to end," Noah said as they walked up the stairs. He would see her to her bedchamber and then continue to his own – although there was a good chance that one of them would sneak into the room of the other once all were abed. "It shall be interesting to see what my brother does with all of this."

"Yes," Percy said, wishing she could tell Noah more but remembering her promise to Faith. "He has an interest in Faith, does he not?"

"He does," Noah said with a chuckle. "He will not speak much of it, however. I believe he told her once that he intended to marry her, and for whatever reason, she was not pleased with his pursuit."

"And yet," Percy mused, "neither one of them has yet married another."

"No, not yet," Noah said, "although Eric seems to have plenty of ladies to keep him company."

"But not Faith."

"No, not Lady Faith."

"Well," she said when they came to her door as she turned and wrapped her arms around his neck. "I am most happy that is not something of which to worry myself over. For I have found my love and we will never hide it from one another again."

"Never," he promised. "I love you, Percy."

"And I love you, Noah," she said.

"Who would have thought when we began this crazy treasure hunt that it would unlock the key to my heart?"

"Who would have thought," she mused, smiling at him. "Although I could have told you that I was the key a lot earlier had you allowed it."

"If only I had listened," he said ruefully.

"Well, you have trust in us now," she said, planting a kiss on his lips. "And that is all that matters."

EPILOGUE

*P*ercy stood in the doorway of what was going to be their country home, watching Noah as he sat, bent over the desk in front of him. Books were piled high on each side of the desk, and he looked up only to dip his quill pen into the inkwell in front of him, before he began to write once more.

She smiled, crossing her arms as she watched him, so deep in concentration, her heart near to bursting in love and pride. At home, when he focused on anything in his life, he put his entire soul into it and became unstoppable.

He stilled, looking up, placing his pen down carefully when he saw her.

"Percy," he said, pushing back his chair and walking over to her. He dove his hands into her hair, lifting it back away from her face before he leaned down and kissed her.

"When did you return home?"

"Just a few minutes ago," she said with a smile. "We had a great deal of fun now that Madeline is home."

"I'm glad to hear it," he said, resting his forehead against hers.

"Noah?"

"Yes?"

"Are you ready?"

"For... oh goodness."

Percy began to laugh as Noah's face turned from tranquil to shocked to horrified.

"I must prepare myself."

"Not to worry. I guessed you had likely become rather involved in your books, so I came to remind you with a few hours to spare. The men will be here to collect you soon."

"Should we be together right now?"

"Likely not unchaperoned," she agreed. "But does it really matter? It shall be a wonderful day, with only the people who matter the most in the world around us."

He placed a quick kiss on her lips before wrapping his arm around her waist and walking her out of the room. "All that is important are the promises we will make to one another."

"Agreed," Percy said, smiling up at him.

"Where is everyone else?"

"Most are preparing themselves for the festivities tonight and the wedding tomorrow morning, I believe."

Their country home was not nearly as large as the one Eric would call home, but it was perfect for them, and contained just enough bedrooms that they were able to host those who meant the most to them.

"Are your cousins coming?"

"My aunt is attending alone," she said. "Apparently, Elizabeth is far too busy preparing for a wedding of her own."

"Oh, yes, with Lord Stephen, that's right," Noah said with a chuckle. "Well, that all worked out for the best."

"It most certainly did," she said earnestly, leaning toward him to give him a kiss.

"I shall see you soon," he said, leaving her at the chamber she was calling her own for just one more night.

"See you soon," she whispered, placing a quick kiss on his lips.

The night passed with both dizzying speed and also seemed to drag on as Percy couldn't help but both anticipate and dread the event to come the next morning. She could not wait for what followed, but she had always so despised the formality and contrived ceremony. She supposed she would just have to get through it, knowing what awaited her on the other side.

They had decided to be married at the small chapel near their country home, both of them wishing they could do this with just the two of them but knowing that their closest of friends and family would choose to be a part of their day.

As Percy stepped through the doorway of the wooden chapel, its usual mustiness somewhat dispersed with the airing out over the past few days, all she could see was Noah, standing there, rather uncomfortably, near the altar.

And suddenly, everything changed. She nearly floated up to him, and as the vicar read the words that she had turned her nose up at before, they filled her heart, and she knew then, with absolute certainty, that it wasn't about the ceremony or how they chose to commit their lives to one another – it was rather, the fact that they were doing so with love for one another deep in their hearts.

As they were proclaimed husband and wife, Noah, the ever-steady rule follower, leaned in and kissed her without prompt, sealing the promise they had made.

Percy leaned back, looked up into those eyes that she knew would love her forever, and she grinned.

Noah's brows lifted as he stared at her, the two of them in their own world together, oblivious to those who were beginning to surround them, expectantly waiting.

"Noah," she said. "I love weddings."

"You do?"

"I do," she said resolutely. "And more importantly – I love you most of all."

* * *

Dear reader,

I hope you enjoyed Percy and Noah's story as they searched for the next clue and unexpectedly found one another. I appreciate you travelling to Bath with me and discovering all that it has to offer.

We've gotten to know Faith over the past few books, and as much as she is determined to be single forever, can Eric, Lord Ferrington, bring down all of her walls? Find out in the grumpy vs sunshine, one bed only, forced proximity romance, The Lord's Compass.

If you haven't yet signed up for my newsletter, I would love to have you join! You will receive Unmasking a Duke for free, as well as links to giveaways, sales, new releases, and stories about my coffee addiction, my struggle to keep my plants alive, and how much trouble one loveable wolf-looka-like dog can get into.

www.elliestclair.com/ellies-newsletter

You will also receive links to giveaways, sales, updates, launch information, promos, and the newest recommended reads.

Or you can join my Facebook group, Ellie St. Clair's Ever Afters, and stay in touch daily.

Happy reading!

Ellie

* * *

The Lord's Compass
Reckless Rogues, Book 4

Will forced proximity turn these enemies to lovers or only cause an arranged marriage of resentment?

Eric Rowley, Earl of Ferrington, is a roguish charmer, but only one woman will ever own his heart - Lady Faith Embury. Despite her sharp-tongued insults, Eric can't help but be drawn to her. When he agrees to undertake an adventurous quest to help his friend, the only thing he will miss is the woman he loves – and not the life of responsibility he is leaving behind.

Faith will never forgive, and never forget what Eric did, but nor can she move on. For there is only one man who has ever stirred her heart, but she can never trust him again. This means she has no confidence in him to do what is required to solve the next clue in her friends' treasure hunt. The only way to ensure success is to tag along herself.

When Eric discovers his stowaway, he is both delighted and perturbed. For their forced proximity is sure to mean ruin, and he isn't sure that she will ever agree to an arranged marriage – even though she is all he ever wanted.

This is an enemies-to-lovers, second chance, arranged marriage, he-falls-first Regency romance featuring a stubborn heroine and an audacious hero.

THE LORD'S COMPASS - CHAPTER ONE

1806 ~ KENT, ENGLAND

*E*ric had no idea where he was going.

Did he own this estate? Yes, in a sense. It was one of a few that his family had obtained over the many years of the storied Rowley history that his father had been so keen on sharing with him. Eric, however, did not need multiple estates and therefore had gifted it to his brother and his new bride as it was perfect for Noah and he had no desire for it himself.

It was not as though he had spent an overly great amount of time here. He had grown up on his family's entailed estate, Hollingsworth. He was lord there now that his father had passed, although his mother ran the place. He knew he should take on the responsibility, but the truth was, it was far easier for him this way.

He wondered now if these gardens he found himself in were supposed to be a maze, or if the hedges had grown that way over time.

Now, he had no idea how to return to the festivities. He supposed if he wandered long enough, he'd eventually find his way back.

His brother's wedding had occurred just that morning, and he had never seen Noah as happy as he was today.

Despite the bride and groom disappearing for a time, the small party had continued to celebrate the marriage. Eric had led them until he had decided to take to the gardens to smoke his cheroot away from everyone else as the ladies were not fond of the smoke.

Then a little wandering had led to his current situation.

"How in the hell did I end up here?" he mused, scratching his temple and turning around in a circle. He looked up, seeing the house rising in the distance, seemingly grinning down at him mockingly. It should be... north? Directions had always confused him. He had tried multiple times now to make his way toward the house and reached a dead end with every attempt.

Suddenly he heard a snap and a whistle right next to his ear before an arrow hit a target ahead and to the right of him with a thud. He had enough wherewithal to notice that it lodged directly in the center.

"Having trouble?"

He whirled around at the voice, both surprised and pleased to find Lady Faith Embury standing twenty yards away across the grass, watching him with amusement in her blue eyes, her face, with its high cheekbones and well-defined jawline, otherwise expressionless, her arms crossed through a bow in front of her.

"Not at all," he said, lifting his chin. "Simply enjoying some afternoon air."

"I can smell the smoke from here," she said, wrinkling her nose, and Eric would have laughed if he wasn't awestruck by his presence. She was a tall woman, as strong physically as she was within, but she held herself with such confidence that he had never been able to resist the pull toward her – one that caused him such vexation.

He threw down the nearly finished cheroot and extinguished it with his foot, snapping his heel before clasping his hands behind his back and walking toward her.

"Did you need a break from all of your dancing?" she asked, tilting her head to the side, her smile as brittle as the sarcasm that dripped from her words.

"You were watching me?" he asked with a grin that he knew would only serve to annoy her, but he couldn't seem to help himself from pestering her.

She shifted slightly from one foot to the other, enough to show that he had irked her, and he couldn't contain his pleasure that he had achieved his goal.

"You're rather hard to miss, the way you flit from woman to woman," she said, lifting her nose in the air. "Half the women in there are married. Or does that not concern you?"

He reached out and took her bow, running his fingers over the fine wood as he examined it, wishing it was her soft skin he was touching so intimately instead.

"You're jealous."

"I am most certainly not!" she said hotly, crossing her arms over her chest as though warding him away.

"Believe that if you want," he said, leaning down and tucking a piece of her dark blond hair behind her ear. "But we both know the truth."

"You're impossible," she said, turning her head to the side.

"Not impossible. I am correct. Always am on these things," he said, reaching out to tap her nose, and she slapped his hand away.

"Do not touch me."

"I thought you liked it when I touched you."

"I did once. But that was before."

"Before what?" he asked, genuinely wanting to know. He had waited two years to learn what had caused her interest in him to turn to such disdain.

"You know very well to what I am referring."

"Actually," he retorted, "I do not. Are you ready to talk about our kiss yet or do you need another year or two?"

She whipped her head from one side to the other as though to make sure that no one could hear them, and Eric couldn't help but chuckle.

"I doubt there is anyone within hearing distance. What *are* you doing out here alone shooting arrows during a party, anyway?"

He knew how much she enjoyed archery, and while they had all participated in the sport yesterday, now was rather odd timing for it.

"I needed time alone."

"You are not exactly dressed for it," he said, using his words as an excuse to run his eyes up and down her body, appreciating her lean form and the strength in her arms.

"My attire is none of your concern. As it happens, I am surprised you would remember our… kiss. Is such an act not a frequent occurrence in your life?" she asked, raising a brow, but he could tell that she was interested in his answer – and slightly flustered at this turn of conversation, if the pinkish hue rising in her cheeks was any indication.

"I am not the rake you think I am."

"No?"

"Not at all."

"Then why does every woman who mentions your name do so with a smile on her face and a twinkle in her eye?" she asked, the hostility remaining.

"Because of my wit and charm," he said, grinning again as he loved teasing her.

"Mm-hmm."

She turned in a swirl of silver skirts, picked up her quiver and walked over to the target, from which she plucked five arrows, all gathered near the center of the target. At least now he had a better idea of where he was. How had he not recognized the course? He really must be more observant.

"Are you ready to return?" he asked, and, despite her height, she still had to tilt her head back to look up at him, her crystal blue eyes vibrant beneath her lashes.

Suddenly they blinked and looked around them before returning to his face.

"You are lost," she said, the realization dawning, inspiration striking her face as she looked around them, the first hint of a smile tugging at her lips. "You do not know how to return, do you?"

"Of course I do!" he said indignantly. "I own this place. At least, I did until recently."

"And yet you cannot find your way back." She let out a slight chortle of glee.

"I can."

"Prove it."

"What?"

"Prove that you know how to return to the house," she said, stepping closer to him.

"How do you suggest I do that?"

"Very simply. Lead us back," she said, waving her arm forward. "I am ready to return."

She lifted the quiver of arrows onto her back and slid the bow onto her arm.

"I will carry those for you," he said, holding his hands out.

"It is fine."

"No," he said with a pointed stare. "It is not. How would it look if I returned with you carrying everything and me alone?"

Her mirth quickly took a turn to annoyance once more.

"That is your concern? How it would look to others?"

Goodness, she was beautiful when she was all fired up like this. He just wished it wasn't in such anger towards him. She hadn't always been like this. She used to be much sweeter, and would allow him lenience she didn't to any others. But everything had changed between them now, and the vibrant charm of before had transformed into ire that always appeared to be directed toward him.

"Just give me the bag," he said, holding his arm out, and she reluctantly slid it off her shoulders and passed it to him.

"It's called a quiver."

"I know."

He set his feet toward the house and paused, looking over to her, needing her to lead but determined not to tell her so.

She rolled her eyes and shook her head. "This way," she said, pointing down the path to the right.

"I know the way."

"Lord Ferrington, everyone knows that you should not be out wandering alone. I wish you would realize it as well."

"I am not a child."

"Are you not?"

"No," he said indignantly, "of course not."

For the first time, however, her words unsettled him. For as rude as she had been to him over the past two years, they had never had the opportunity for such a long conversation alone. She had made sure of it.

Now that they had, he wondered if their relationship should have remained as it was – distant.

* * *

FAITH HATED how much he disconcerted her.

As he walked beside her, her quiver on his back, she

became increasingly annoyed at how much his presence affected her.

There was a good few feet between them, and yet it seemed as though she could sense the heat from his body radiating across the short distance. He had always had such magnetism. It was more than the size of his body. It was the way he carried himself, the heartiness of his laughter, his ability to say what he thought without restriction.

He was everything she wanted to be.

And everything she could have had if only things had been different.

But the man he was – the flirt, the charmer – was the very reason they were not together. For she was selfish. She knew that. She didn't like sharing – most especially him.

Which was why she tried to distance herself from him, for seeing him with other women only made everything worse.

"I know where we are now," he said as they turned onto the path toward the house.

"I should hope so," she said wryly. "This takes you straight to the terrace."

"Where would you like me to take your bow and arrows?"

"I can take them from here," she said, holding out her hands, but he shook his head, his dark hair, too long for the style of the day, but of course annoyingly charming on him, sliding over his forehead.

"I am far too much of a gentleman to allow you to do so."

"Oh, you are a gentleman now?"

"Always have been," he said jovially, his devilish dimples deepening. "That's what the title of an earl gets you."

She rolled her eyes and turned toward the stables. "One of the stableboys can take care of them," she said, and he followed.

THE SCHOLAR'S KEY

"As you wish," he said. "Now tell me, why did you leave the party?"

"I am not much one for parties," she said, keeping her gaze ahead so that he wouldn't read the lie in her eyes. But the truth was far worse – for the truth was, she hadn't been able to stop herself from watching him flirt with Percy's cousin, Lady Rebecca.

It had tugged at her heart, especially after what she had thought was a moment between her and Eric during the wedding ceremony. As her closest friend, Lady Persephone Holloway, had married Eric's brother, Noah, she had stood beside her as her bridesmaid while Eric had been his best man. She hadn't been able to take her eyes off of him as the clergyman read the words tying the married couple together.

And she had hated herself for it.

Of course, to him a longing gaze was nothing.

She was a fool.

But she had known that for some time.

"I remember one party you seemed to particularly enjoy," he said, wiggling his eyebrows.

Her spine stiffened.

"You think quite highly of yourself, Lord Ferrington," she said tersely.

"Faith, there is no need to be so formal."

"There are many reasons to be formal, my lord."

"Faith—"

"Lady Faith."

He sighed, the first sign of his cheeriness slipping.

"Lady Faith, then."

He stopped as they neared the stables, turning to stand in front of her. His full lips were pressed into a line as his hazel eyes stared into hers. "What happened, Faith? What changed?"

She stared at him. She had told herself she would never

speak of this, but perhaps this is what she needed – what they both needed to close this door.

"I saw you with her."

He flinched backward at the intensity of her tone, although his mask of confession remained.

"With whom?"

"The other woman. That night."

"Faith, I do not know who you mean, there was no—"

He stopped abruptly, his eyes widening as, apparently, his memory restored itself.

"Another woman… you saw that?"

"I did," she said, stepping forward, snatching her quiver from his grasp, which had slackened in his surprise at her revelation. "Which is why there will never be such thing as you and me again."

Keep reading The Lord's Compass!

ALSO BY ELLIE ST. CLAIR

Christmas Books
A Match Made at Christmas
A Match Made in Winter

Christmastide with His Countess
Her Christmas Wish
Merry Misrule
Duke of Christmas
Duncan's Christmas

Reckless Rogues
The Earls's Secret
The Viscount's Code
The Scholar's Key
The Lord's Compass
Prequel, The Duke's Treasure, available in:
I Like Big Dukes and I Cannot Lie

The Remingtons of the Regency
The Mystery of the Debonair Duke
The Secret of the Dashing Detective
The Clue of the Brilliant Bastard
The Quest of the Reclusive Rogue

The Unconventional Ladies
Lady of Mystery

Lady of Fortune

Lady of Providence

Lady of Charade

The Unconventional Ladies Box Set

To the Time of the Highlanders

A Time to Wed

A Time to Love

A Time to Dream

Thieves of Desire

The Art of Stealing a Duke's Heart

A Jewel for the Taking

A Prize Worth Fighting For

Gambling for the Lost Lord's Love

Romance of a Robbery

Thieves of Desire Box Set

The Bluestocking Scandals

Designs on a Duke

Inventing the Viscount

Discovering the Baron

The Valet Experiment

Writing the Rake

Risking the Detective

A Noble Excavation

A Gentleman of Mystery

The Bluestocking Scandals Box Set: Books 1-4

The Bluestocking Scandals Box Set: Books 5-8

Blooming Brides
A Duke for Daisy
A Marquess for Marigold
An Earl for Iris
A Viscount for Violet

The Blooming Brides Box Set: Books 1-4

Happily Ever After
The Duke She Wished For
Someday Her Duke Will Come
Once Upon a Duke's Dream
He's a Duke, But I Love Him
Loved by the Viscount
Because the Earl Loved Me

Happily Ever After Box Set Books 1-3
Happily Ever After Box Set Books 4-6

The Victorian Highlanders
Duncan's Christmas - (prequel)
Callum's Vow
Finlay's Duty
Adam's Call
Roderick's Purpose
Peggy's Love

The Victorian Highlanders Box Set Books 1-5

Searching Hearts

Duke of Christmas (prequel)

Quest of Honor

Clue of Affection

Hearts of Trust

Hope of Romance

Promise of Redemption

Searching Hearts Box Set (Books 1-5)

Standalones

Always Your Love

The Stormswept Stowaway

A Touch of Temptation

For a full list of all of Ellie's books, please see www.elliestclair.com/books.

ABOUT THE AUTHOR

Ellie has always loved reading, writing, and history. For many years she has written short stories, non-fiction, and has worked on her true love and passion -- romance novels.

In every era there is the chance for romance, and Ellie enjoys exploring many different time periods, cultures, and geographic locations. No matter when or where, love can always prevail. She has a particular soft spot for the bad boys of history, and loves a strong heroine in her stories.

Ellie and her husband love nothing more than spending time at home with their children and Husky cross. Ellie can typically be found at the lake in the summer, pushing the stroller all year round, and, of course, with her computer in her lap or a book in hand.

She also loves corresponding with readers, so be sure to contact her!

www.elliestclair.com
ellie@elliestclair.com

- facebook.com/elliestclairauthor
- x.com/ellie_stclair
- instagram.com/elliestclairauthor
- amazon.com/author/elliestclair
- goodreads.com/elliestclair
- bookbub.com/authors/elliest.clair
- pinterest.com/elliestclair

Printed in Great Britain
by Amazon